Flashy Fiction 2

AND OTHER INSANE TALES

(An anthology of the strange, bizarre and just plain weird)

JEN WYLIE
SEAN HAYDEN

Untold
Press

FLASHY FICTION AND OTHER INSANE TALES 2

An Untold Press Anthology
First Printing, March 2013

Published by Untold Press LLC
114 NE Estia Lane
Port St Lucie, FL 34983
www.untoldpress.com

ISBN: 978-0615772912

PRODUCED IN THE UNITED STATES OF AMERICA

10 9 8 7 6 5 4 3 2 1

Dedication

From Both of Us

To the quiet ones, the trodden on, the kids in the hall
The wolves in sheep's clothing, fooling them all.
To the Goth, the dark, and the utterly strange
The bizarre, the mutants, and the strangely deranged
To the clinically insane and those not yet diagnosed
Even un-medicated, you understand us the most
This Flashy's for you

Contents

Fireflies

by

Jen Wylie

Aggie wasn't overly upset when she opened her eyes and found she wasn't in bed. Of course, what the hospital considered a bed didn't exactly fit her description. After she turned ninety she stopped caring about a lot of things, but having a comfortable bed so her aching bones could have a good rest remained on the list.

She was a little put out she hadn't made it to a century. She'd been so close, too. It was just another few weeks until her birthday. Still, ninety-nine was good enough, a lot longer than most people lived. It wasn't until the last few months she'd gone downhill and had a rough time of it.

Machines were blaring in the poorly lit room. She watched nurses run in, then doctors, and eventually her family came as well. She smiled down at them, happy to see they were saddened by her passing but not emotional wrecks. Everyone knew it was coming, even her.

Dying hadn't been so bad. She'd gone in her sleep, which suited her just fine. Now…

A frown crossed her wrinkled face. *Now what?* She'd been raised, and lived, a devote Catholic.

"Where's that light?" She turned, and smiled. Well, there it was, hiding behind her. There should have been trumpets or angels singing or something to let her know it was there. She was almost a hundred for goodness sake.

Once she saw it she felt the pull and smiled as her spirit drifted toward it. Relief flooded her. There was a light! All those damn atheists were wrong! Not that she ever had any doubt.

She spread her arms and closed her eyes as she drew closer. The brightness was blinding. Warmth wrapped around her as she entered the light. It encircled her, filling her with peace and joy. Everything was perfect. She had lived a full and good life.

She had no idea how long she stayed wrapped in peace. Aggie didn't particularly care either. She'd come home. Peace was her reward.

After a time she did open her eyes. Bright light still surrounded her. Her frown returned. *Where is the tunnel? The angels? How do I get to Heaven?*

Worry began to seep into her peaceful thoughts. Had she done something wrong? Before panic could set in, the light began to change.

It dimmed, becoming not so blinding. The peace and warmth still remained, wrapping her in its comfort. For that she was thankful, it kept her calm as the light began to slowly spin. She blinked and let out a sigh. The tunnel of light. Finally she was heading down it. All around her faint images came and went. At first she thought they were the souls of others who had gone on before her. Finally she realized they were, in fact, her memories.

"My life is flashing before my eyes," she said with a chuckle. "I'll be here a while." She settled into the warmth and happily watched the memories forming around her. Most of them were good ones. Many she'd almost forgotten.

Time passed, or so she assumed, she really had no idea. The memories finally slowed and then strangely sped up again, spinning around her faster and faster. They moved so fast they made her dizzy. The images zipped by and blurred together. They tightened around her, pushing against the light. She gasped, trying not to be afraid. The tightening increased, but it didn't hurt. She relaxed and closed her eyes. Pressure pushed at her from all sides, building and building until suddenly…it was gone.

She opened her eyes. The memories had disappeared, leaving her in a tunnel of light.

"Now the angels and heaven."

She smiled and waited.

Waited.

Waited.

Not knowing how much time passed started to truly make her cranky. She wasn't getting any younger…

She laughed. She wasn't getting any older either. Not anymore. Patience was a virtue. Perhaps this was a test of that. So she waited some more, and grew terribly bored.

The tunnel of light didn't change, there was nothing to see or do. No scents tickled her nose and absolute silence filled the space around her. She didn't even have the sounds of her heartbeat or breathing to distract her.

Hello?

Her eyes opened wide. No sound had come from her lips. Her query remained within her.

She found it very hard not to panic. Death wasn't supposed to be like this, was it? Her old brain struggled with everything that had happened so far. She'd died and then become a spirit. There had been a bright light and a tunnel. All of those incidents fit with what she'd expected. Even the flashbacks of memory sort of did, the images of people could have been what near death experiences described of meeting those who'd gone beyond.

She wanted angels though. The pearly gates and God and heaven. She'd prayed and been a good person all of her life. Certainly she deserved paradise?

Didn't she? The events so far made her pause and think harder. She concentrated and went over her memories again and again. So intent on finding something, she didn't notice her surroundings changing at first.

Lights filled the tunnel now. No, they were the tunnel. Thousands of them, maybe more. As she watched in fascination they moved around her, or perhaps she moved amidst them. From tiny specks to radiant balls they floated in every direction. Some were pure white, others golden, and the rest ranged in color from one end of the rainbow to the other.

The sight was beautiful. If she'd been able, she would have cried. She was one of the lights.

What color am I?

They continued to move and swirl about. Eventually she discovered if she concentrated and focused on a light she could move closer to it. Flitting about she found it both calming and peaceful to be part of a sea of light.

Fireflies. That's what they all reminded her of. Millions and millions of fireflies.

She'd chased the little lightening bugs as a child, catching them and sealing them in her mother's old mason jars. She taught her children to catch them as well, and then her grandchildren. Last summer, she even had the joy of sharing them with her great grandchildren. Everyone loved the chasing and catching. The challenge of getting them into the jars without letting the others out always brought fits of laughter. Afterward, tired and happy, they would watch the bugs dance within the jar until bedtime.

Happiness filled her at the memories. Her glow became brighter, more vibrant and joyful. Something pulled her and she floated passed other lights before once again slowing.

Light filled her vision. Awestruck, she stared at the swirling mass she was a part of. Millions of lights spun. They seemed never ending, rising far above and below in a swirling vortex of rainbows.

The sight was beyond description, beyond words. Everything was just so…big. Beauty didn't describe it. She watched, transfixed at the lights, then she noticed some were falling.

They flew from the spinning outer ring into the center where they swirled down and down and down creating a rain of multihued stars.

She felt once again young, free. The weight of her ninety-nine years melted away. Everything which had held her back, kept her from being pure and true, disappeared in a drift of light. She remained Aggie, but was both more and less.

One of a million, million beacons of light she floated, thoughts of what she should have gone on to not forgotten, but now she just didn't care. This was more. This was…everything. Eternal. Beautiful. Wondrous.

Like fireflies, we are. Lighting the heavens.

Something tugged her then, an invisible force, pulling her toward the empty center. Her speed increased until she flung free from the spinning multitude of lights. Euphoria and freedom encompassed her as she fell swirling down and down.

There are so many of them…so many like me…

She fell, the lights becoming fewer as they drifted here and there over the world. The light disappeared into darkness.

There was no fear. Not from the familiar night sounds. Not from this dark. Nighttime wasn't pure darkness. There were little lights here and there. Lights like her.

She flew, happy and free, keeping back the darkness in her own little way.

"Mommy, look! There's another one! Look!"

"I see it, sweetie. Quick! Hurry and catch it. Jimmy, get the jar ready!"

Fireflies

Flashy Fiction and Other Insane Tales was barely out before Sean and I started talking about doing a second one. It was so much fun we both agreed right away. Of course, actually finding time to write was another matter entirely. I came up with the idea of doing a challenge. Sitting outside one lovely evening I wondered when the fireflies would start to come out again. I looove fireflies! The proverbial light bulb went off then, and I ran inside to challenge Sean. We had two days to each write a story, whatever we wanted, as long as there were fireflies in it (and it was paranormal). That is how this story came to be.

~Jen

Security

by

Sean Hayden

Security

Maggie caught the glowing bug in her tiny little hand. Even though she had only seen ten summers, she remembered catching them every year. "Firefry time," she had always called it. Some of her happiest memories surrounded catching multitudes of the diminutive bugs, putting them in a jar lined with grass she had ripped out of the ground herself, and keeping them on the nightstand by her bed. For hours she'd watch their tiny beacons glow next to her while she drifted off to sleep.

This year was a little different. Her whole life had been uprooted and destroyed as far as she was concerned. It all started six months ago when her mother left to pursue a career in the fashion industry. Instead of asking her father to find a new job, she decided she'd be better off alone. Her father received the divorce papers a month later. Two months after that he took Maggie and moved back to Wisconsin.

Maggie missed Chicago. They had lived in the suburbs and had a huge back yard with massive pine and willow trees. She would spend hours out there collecting lightning bugs and running barefoot through the soft grass. She missed her friends, she missed her school, and she missed her life. About the only thing she didn't miss was her mother. Maggie still couldn't believe she had abandoned them for a job.

Thinking about her mother caused an involuntary muscle spasm in her hand. Maggie gasped, remembering the poor firefly trapped in her palm. Wincing, she slowly opened her hand. The tiny bug was alive but had seen better days. Its wings were crumpled and one of its legs didn't look very healthy either. "Oh, no! I'm so sorry, little guy."

She wandered over to the tangled mess of raspberry bushes next to the cabin. Maggie's dad had been a construction worker in Chicago. With her mother gone, he couldn't afford to pay the mortgage, the bills, and keep them clothed and fed. He owned a medium sized cabin about thirty miles outside of Madison that he had built himself. It didn't have a mortgage, used little electricity, and had a well of the coldest, purest spring water she had ever tasted. As a family they would vacation here a few weeks out of the year. She loved it. The wooded area around the cabin was a never ending source of exploration.

She never expected her father to sell their house and walk away with almost nothing. They moved in, he found a job rather quickly with a local construction company, mother was gone, and life moved on. At least Maggie still had her fireflies.

Not having the heart to stuff the poor injured little fellow in a jar, she did the next best thing. She put her hand next to a raspberry bush leaf, carefully avoiding the sharp thorns that came along with it. Using the finger of her other hand, she gently nudged the injured bug onto the leaf before running off to find healthier specimens.

"Mags, time for bed, angel."

Her hand clasped gently around the last lighting bug of the night. "Coming, Daddy!"

She ran back to the back patio. Holding her treasure in her hand, she carefully unscrewed the cap of the glass mason jar sitting on the old wrought iron table. She lifted the lid off and flipped her last catch inside, quickly replacing it before the other three escaped. She sighed. Back home she would have had twenty by now. It surprised her how few lighting bugs were in the heavily wooded area. Maybe it was just a little too early into "firefry season".

She clutched the jar to her chest and ran for the door. Her father ruffled her hair as she passed.

"Hi, Daddy."

"Hi, Bug. Catch lots?"

She stopped and held up her jar. "Not really, only four. Well five, but I sorta crushed one. I let him go."

"Don't worry, you'll catch more tomorrow," he said and shut the door. "I have an early day tomorrow, but Mrs. Tomlin will be here. Want me to say goodbye before I go?"

"Of course! I'd be sad if you left without saying goodbye." She tried to keep the fear out of her voice. Panic seized her as the thought of her father leaving like her mother had left flittered across her thoughts.

Her father noticed and regretted even asking. He hated waking her up early, but she insisted on it every day. He had a feeling he knew why, too. For the hundredth time that day, he cursed his ex.

He bent down and hugged his daughter. "Then of course I will. I love you, Mags. I'm never going to leave, I promise."

She pulled back. "I know, Dad. Now you go to bed, too," she said and smiled before heading to her room.

She closed the door behind her and set the jar down next to her bed before changing into her jammies. She flipped the light switch and jumped into bed to watch the light show. Like magic, the bugs started glowing one by one. A small smile crept onto Maggie's face as she felt herself drifting off to sleep.

A bright light woke her sometime later. She opened her eyes and saw the light from her firefly jar glowing brighter than usual. "Huh, it's purple," she whispered and closed her eyes again, rolling over to face the wall behind her. The sound of tapping on glass woke her up fully. She turned and looked again at the jar of fireflies.

Three of them lie dead on the bottom of the jar, missing hunks of soft chitin, their glowing fluids smeared on the inside of the jar. Pounding on the glass was the fourth, only it wasn't a firefly. Maggie gasped at the purple winged creature. It looked almost like a little girl with butterfly wings. Her tiny hand smashed against the glass in fury. Her eyes blazed with purple fire that matched the lavender glow of her wings. Hatred poured through the glass like heat.

"Wha–what are you?"

"You know what I am! Now let me out of this jar!"

Maggie reached a trembling hand toward the rocking prison. The faerie licked her lips in anticipation of freedom, and flesh. "You won't hurt me?"

"Of course not! I only want to be free. Now open this jar immediately!"

Maggie nodded and grabbed the jar. She slid out of bed and walked over to the window in her room. She had no intention of releasing it inside. She set it down on the sill and lifted on the heavy glass. It clicked three times and she held the jar outside, unscrewing the lid.

The faerie bolted from her prison and drew a tiny dagger from the belt around her waist. With a squeal of glee, it spun and slashed at Maggie's hand.

She screamed, dropped the jar, and fell to the hardwood floor beneath her. Closing her eyes, she flailed her arms. The faerie wasn't done. It latched onto her hand and bit deeply into Maggie's finger, moaning as the blood hit her tongue. In pain, Maggie jerked her hand, sending the faerie flying out the window with a piece of her flesh in its mouth.

Not to be cheated from delivering retribution on its captor, it flew back toward Maggie. Just as it tried to go through the open window, Maggie got to her knees and slammed it shut. The faerie screeched and frantically beat its wings backward. Her body had already cleared the opening as the window slammed down, pinning its wings and crushing them. It screamed in agony.

Maggie sat on her feet watching the struggling faerie. Its screaming died into helpless agonizing sobs. Even though it had attacked her, she felt bad for the tiny creature. "I'm sorry," she said softly.

The fairy looked up in shock. "You're sorry? You trap me in a jar, crush my wings, sit there and watch me suffer…and you're sorry?"

"I didn't mean to crush your wings. I didn't want you to bite me again. I was trying to lock you outside."

"Free me then."

Maggie nodded and got back up on her knees. She scooted forward and touched the window. "You won't attack me again?"

"No. I won't attack you, young one."

Maggie thought she could see honesty on the faerie's face and nodded. She lifted the window and the faerie dropped to the floor, landing on its hands and knees. Maggie lifted the window until it stayed open. "Will you be able to fly?"

"We are magic itself. I will heal, but it will take a few moments."

Maggie nodded and sat down with her back against the wall. "I really am sorry. I didn't mean to hurt you."

"I'm sorry I bit you. Most humans we meet, seek only to destroy. We're used to defending ourselves. Have no fear. I call truce. You shall be safe from me and my kind forever."

"Thank you. Would you like me to sit you on the window sill?"

"Just like that? You forgive me and release me?"

Maggie nodded. So did the faerie. Gently, Maggie lowered her hand on the floor next to her. Gingerly, the faerie crawled into her palm. Maggie slowly placed her hand near the sill and let the creature climb off her hand. It stood, shook out its wings, and glowed brightly with its hazy purple light. Maggie saw the wings straighten and heal right before her eyes.

Maggie stood and backed away, letting the faerie leave. It fluttered its wings and hovered by the window. "I cannot accept my freedom without giving you something in return. What is your wish?"

Maggie thought about it. There was only one thing in the whole world she wanted. Security. "Don't ever let my daddy leave me."

"Done," she said and flew out the window, quickly fading from sight.

Maggie woke with a feeling of terror. She sat up and blinked, remembering her daddy left earlier. He kept his promise and woke her up to say goodbye. The foggy memory made her smile. She slid out of bed to go get some breakfast.

She padded softly into the kitchen and saw Mrs. Tomlin on the phone. Her shoulders were shaking and it sounded like she was crying. She didn't hear Maggie behind her, so she listened quietly wondering what had happened.

"How did he die?"

Maggie's heart froze.

"The truck flipped? Oh, my God. I can't believe he's gone. Of course I'll keep an eye on Maggie. Does she have any family left?"

Tears started falling down Maggie's face.

"A mother? Her father said something about her being in New York. I'll have to ask her when she wakes up. I hope I can handle her...she's going to be devastated. Poor, little thing."

Maggie's world exploded. She felt herself falling and she hit the floor hard. The sound of the telephone hitting the floor and footsteps filled her ears. "Maggie! Maggie, are you okay?" Mrs. Tomlin's hand lightly slapped Maggie's face.

"The faerie promised. He'd...never...leave."

"Poor thing is delusional." The light slaps turned into a loud crack as the palm of her hand struck the child, trying to snap her out of it.

The kitchen door splintered and flew apart. Mrs. Tomlin looked up in horror as a something walked through the doorway. She screamed. It stood over six feet tall and was covered in gore. Eyeless sockets stared at her in hatred. Flesh had been burned crispy around its lips and most of its head. It shambled along the kitchen floor, one leg bent at an impossible angle.

"Get away from my daughter."

"Hey, Sean, know what we should do?"
"What, Jen?"
"We should write more insanely crazy tales for Flashy Fiction and Other Insane Tales Volume 2!"
"Hmmm. That's not a bad idea. When do you want to start?"
"Now!"

And thus was born this book. We, and by we, I mean Jen, thought it would be fun to do a couple of stories with the same topic and see how different the stories turned out. As you can see, they turned out insanely different!

~Sean

Just a Bear

by

Jen Wylie

Jen Wylie

He could smell his sister before he heard her. Coffee and donuts. She came every weeknight after the final shift at the local shop ended, smelling like the place and carrying a bag of end of the day leftovers for their mother.

"How's he doing?"

He grimaced at her whisper. Everyone always whispered here, either that or cried. He'd grown quite sick of both sounds. A strangled noise escaped his throat when he tried to laugh.

Sick. Yes he was very sick, wasn't he?

"Ryan!" Mom grabbed his wrist, leaning in close. "You need some water, sweetie?"

He shook his head slightly, not bothering to open his eyes. The light hurt them too much.

Everything hurt too much, but he'd gotten past the point of complaining about it. He was fifteen and had both feet planted on Death's doorstep. It sucked, but there wasn't a thing he could do about it. There wasn't anything anyone could do, god knows they'd tried. Sometimes, most of the time, the "Big C" won. You could fight it for a while, like he had done, and that gave you hope. He'd first been diagnosed when he was six. He'd almost died then, but had a miraculous, sudden recovery. They'd thought it was gone.

They'd been wrong of course, and here he was again. He didn't delude himself into thinking he'd be lucky twice.

"Is he awake?"

He cracked his eyes open. "I am."

"Ryan didn't have a very good day."

He watched his mother's fingers flutter like little butterflies over her lips as she held in tears. She knew he hated to see her cry.

Janey cleared her throat and sat down on the edge of his bed. She fiddled with the sweater she had on over her uniform, searching for something to say. "Everyone's still asking about you at school. Marty says hey and that he'll be in this weekend."

He smiled a bit. Marty had been his best friend since kindergarten.

The old man across from him groaned in his sleep. It was nearly midnight, and the other five patients in his room were asleep already. Mount Sanders Memorial wasn't a huge hospital, though it was big enough to boast a cancer ward. It was the best in the area though, even if the ward was considered small compared to some, and didn't have a separate area for teens.

Janey chuckled suddenly and both he and Mom stared at her. She gestured toward the old man. "The bear, sorry. He seems a bit old for one of those."

He shifted slightly to look around her and spotted the good sized teddy bear sitting on the man's nightstand. He remembered a younger woman had brought it in for him earlier. The old man hadn't been overly impressed with it either.

"I think it was meant to cheer him up," his mother said reprovingly.

Janey snorted. "It's from the gift shop downstairs. Not a lot of thought put into it."

"I haven't been in there yet," Mom said absently.

"It sucks. Like, that's the only bear they have. Mostly there are flowers and magazines."

"Don't bring me flowers," he muttered.

Janey laughed. "I won't." She looked down at her watch. "Mom, we better get going."

"Yes, you're right." His mom didn't move though.

"Go on," he whispered. "I'm fine." He worried about her. She taken off work when he'd first gotten sick again, but the bills had piled up fast. Now she was back working again, and had picked up another part time job, too. Between two jobs and spending her remaining time with him, she was exhausted and looked it. Sometimes he wished he'd just hurry up and die so everyone else could get on with their lives.

After a few more minutes his family left. The quite hospital noises murmured around him. He stared across the room at the teddy bear. The lights from one of the old man's monitors gleamed in its beaded eyes.

Before he drifted off to sleep the only thing he could think was luckily the bear sat watching the old man, and not him.

He awoke from a nightmare of teddy bears running around the room attacking each other with mini swords. Blinking his eyes he wondered if the nurse had come and given him his meds already and he hadn't noticed. Usually he didn't have such strange dreams.

The first thing he noticed was the empty bed across from him.

"They took him this morning."

He jumped, wincing as pain shot through his entire body. He glared over at the owner of the soft voice.

Peeping over the foot of his bed was a pale boy clutching a worn old stuffed bear.

"Should you be here?"

The boy made a face and pointed to his bald head. "Duh."

"In this room I mean."

The boy shrugged and glanced toward the door. "Did he have a bear?"

24

Ryan blinked at the quick, out of the blue question. "Did he?"

"Yeah, one from the gift shop."

The boy turned and ran to the old man's curtained off area, searching around. "Where is it?"

"I don't know, I guess they took it away with the rest of his stuff."

The boy sighed and stopped looking. He clutched his own bear tighter. "I guess it doesn't matter. It'd be empty now anyways."

"What?"

"Empty. It got what it wanted."

Ryan struggled and finally managed to sit up a bit. "What are you talking about?"

The boy looked him in the eye. "The bear. It took his soul. It took him down to hell."

Ryan shook his head. This kid must have been on more meds than him.

"You don't believe me."

"Sorry, kid."

"One took Eddie last week. I saw it. Missy's aunt brought her one a few days ago. But I stopped it."

"You did?"

The boy nodded. "I told her it was dangerous. She didn't listen, so I took it, and when I was done they had to get rid of it."

Ryan's lips twitched in amusement as he pictured the kid ripping the poor bear's head off or something. "What did you do?"

"Took it to the bathroom and pooped on it."

Ryan choked and then laughed so hard he thought the pain might kill him, never mind a demon haunted teddy bear.

"Elias!" The screech of the nurse made them both turn to the door.

Elias, who couldn't have been more than eight or nine, swore.

"Oh, my god, kid. Stop," Ryan said, still laughing.

Elias grinned at him and then ducked past the nurse as he rushed from the room.

The nurse apologized and then ran after him. He doubted she'd catch him. His mother came in a few minutes later for a quick visit before work and then he had a joyous day of tests and other fun things they did to you when you were dying.

Of course it would be too much to ask for them to leave him alone. They finally finished just before dinner time. His mother had come and gone when he'd been out, but had left a note before heading to her second job.

He had a new roommate across the way, a pretty young woman in her thirties. Already she had a wall decorated with pictures and cards and half a dozen flower arrangements filled her night stand and a shelf above it.

At least she didn't have any teddy bears.

She might not have, but two days later the man next to him passed away in the midafternoon. Ryan hadn't seen much of him, his curtains were usually closed. After they took him away they left the ugly pastel checkered things open. He didn't fail to notice the gift shop bear.

He stared at it, wondering at the coincidence. The bear looked normal enough, not huge, but not a little one either. It was dark brown, with black plastic eyes and a blue bow tied around its neck.

"Did you kill him?"

The bear didn't answer, but then if what Elias said was true, it was empty now.

Thinking of the boy made him magically appear.

"They got another one."

Ryan turned to look at him. "Back again so soon?"

The boy stuck his tongue out. "They're getting worse. You need to help. I have my room covered, but there's no one here to fight back."

"Yeah, you'll have to be more specific, kid."

Elias held up his own worn bear. "You need one to fight back."

"A bear. That's it?"

"No, stupid. A *special* bear."

"I see. But not from the gift shop."

Elias beamed at him. "Right!" He looked over his shoulder. "See ya!" A few moments after darting out of the room a nurse poked her head in, looked around with a scowl on her face and then left again.

Ryan chuckled. Elias seemed to be giving everyone a hard time. He certainly had a vivid imagination.

His day passed slowly, the tests had slowed down. Though part of him was happy about that, the rest of him was bored to tears. Somehow he got through his family's visits. Only the knowledge tomorrow was Saturday kept him going. Weekends meant visits from school friends.

It wasn't only his friends that stopped by. The next day the entire room seemed to be constantly jammed with people. Apparently the weather had turned a bit nicer and people were in the mood to get out.

Marty came by, and so did Erin and James. He would have been happier except for the number of people coming through the room carrying gifts for the other patients. What they held in their hands constantly distracted him. Sometimes there were bears.

Twice, he identified gift shop bears.

Despite knowing he was being an idiot, the bears terrified him. He shouldn't listen to the stories of an eight year kid with cancer. The boy was probably bored and had an overactive imagination.

Still, he couldn't stop thinking about them. It didn't help that the young woman across from him was the recipient of one of the bears. She displayed it proudly...on her nightstand.

"No, no, no," he whispered. "Get rid of it." He shook his head. "Shit."

Pulling his blankets up after the last of his visitors left, he turned toward the door. He needed sleep. Strange dreams had been bothering him, though he couldn't remember what they were. He closed his eyes, trying to push the thought of bears away...

"Ryan! Ryan, baby..."

"Mom, oh god, what should I do?"

The voices of his mom and Janey pulled at him. What were they talking about?

"I'm sorry, Mrs. Tanner. He suddenly took a turn for the worse."

The doctor's voice droned on, lulling him back into oblivion.

Dark, shining black eyes stared at him, pulling him away...

His eyes snapped open suddenly and he reached out blindly. "Janey!"

His sister grasped his hand, and he pulled her in close "I need him. You have to go home..." He gasped for breath, trying to get the words out before it was too late. "Do you remember? Last time? I need him. Please, bring him for me?" He fell back, exhausted.

"Ryan? Shit! What are you talking about? What...oh! Mom, I'll be right back."

"Janey? Janey!"

"I'll be right back!"

Their voices drifted away again, but he smiled. His sister understood.

"Ryan," Janey whispered. "I brought him."

He felt his arm being lifted, something fluffy slipped against him. Smiling softly, he clutched his worn, old bear tightly.

Bright light spread around him. It filled him with warmth and love.

The bear in his arms stared across the room, pulsing its light ever outwards, spreading its protection.

"Wherever did you find that old thing?"

"Shhh, Mom. Look, he's smiling. You remember Pooky Bear. Ryan had him last time. Grampa gave it to him just before he got better. I'd forgotten. I'm glad Ryan remembered."

"It's just a silly old bear."

Ryan continued to smile.

Light flowed from the bear, slipping around Ryan and wrapping him in wings made of light. Its chuckle and voice were heard only by its ward.

Just a bear, am I?

Sean and I once again had a challenge to each write a paranormal story, this time about teddy bears.

For children, their stuffed animals can mean the world to them. Perhaps they really do have something special about them. When I was two, I got a big stuffed cat. It still has a home on my bed. The name Pooky Bear came from my son's favorite bear. This one's for you sweetie.

PS to the emotional readers-sorry for the need for tissues!

~Jen

Mr. McClunkin

by

Sean Hayden

Claudia Withers gazed up at the grayish-brown snowflakes as they fell. They stuck to her face and hair She could feel the fine flecks of soot they deposited as they quickly melted away. She would have to wash her face when she got home. Provided there would be coal enough to heat water for washing. Lately, fuel for the fire had been more than difficult to come by.

Scuffing the toe of her worn leather boot against the slush covered walk, Claudia continued her trek from the factory to her home. Her shift had ended over an hour ago, but the lights of London at Yule enraptured her. At only twelve years, she still had night studies.

She sighed heavily, watching her foggy breath collect in front of her. She hated schoolwork. With the passing of the Standard Education Edict from the Emperor, the children of all the United Empire had to maintain good grades to hold down a job. She couldn't afford not to pass. Her parents relied on her salary as much as their own. Last week her father had slipped and fallen off a structural girder in the new wing of the factory. He'd been forced to take the week off without pay to recuperate. This close to Yule...the festivities would be even more limited for the small family. Claudia didn't mind so much for her sake, but her little brother, Michael, would be very disappointed.

Claudia gasped at the thought of her brother. She had meant to stop by the scrap-yard on the way home to pick up a few more needed pieces for his Yule gift. The yard was across town and she would need to hurry to get there before they closed and locked the gates. She knew the second shift watchman really well, but she doubted he would bend the rules, even for her.

Mr. McClunkin

She ran toward the Seventh Street trolley stop, patting the front of her leather pants as she ran. She hoped she had exact coin to pay for the trip.

She fished out two imperial rupence and dropped them in the palm of the autochauffer's outstretched hand as she boarded the trolley. It closed its mechanical fist around the reddish, coppery coins and croaked a harsh, "Destination, please."

"Oldtowne Scrapyard, please." Claudia waddled carefully down the aisle as the trolley's turbine wound up and it started its chugging journey over the cobblestone streets.

The journey didn't take long and she slipped inside the scrap-yard with minutes to spare.

Ignoring the piles and piles of transport parts, she wound her way to the back where the more delicate pieces ended up. All she needed to finish the gift were two smaller pistons and a rotation collar for the cranial unit. They took longer to find than the journey to the scrap-yard had taken. Even with as much as machines broke down in Imperial London, working parts were becoming hard to come by.

She grabbed her treasures and debated hiding them in her pants. They would wipe out the last of her funds. It was either steal or go hungry for the rest of the week. Her conscience made up her mind for her. Claudia was no thief. She held onto the items proudly and quickly ran to the checkout station.

"Hi, Claudia," Sam said as she approached. He looked at the items in her hand and then up at her face.

"Hi, Sam. This is it," she said and held out the three pieces.

"Couldn't find what you were looking for today, eh?"

He made no motion to punch in the items on the archaic brass register before him. Claudia cocked an eyebrow in puzzlement. "I have these?"

"Yes, smaller parts are hard to come by this close to Yule. Oh, well. Better luck next time," he said and winked.

Understanding dawned on Claudia's face. "Yes. Maybe next time," she said and gave him a huge smile.

She practically ran out the gate and back to the trolley stop. Luck continued to smile upon her as one came chugging to a stop just as she settled in to wait. She smiled and climbed aboard, dropping two more rupence for the journey.

Claudia locked the cranial unit on the body of the mechanical bear. It took her only a few moments to daub enough glue on the pilfered fur that would cover the metallic skull beneath and then slip it on. She held it in place lovingly as it quickly dried. She crinkled her nose at the smell of the glue. She had never liked the acrid odor.

She ran her hand down the back of the bear and found the keyhole. Reaching over she grabbed the heart topped brass winding key and lined it up. She plunged it home and began cranking it relentlessly. After an eternity, it wouldn't wind anymore. She pulled out the key and sat back. The bear's eyes came to life first. Lifeless glass orbs began to glow a fiery red.

The bear leaned over and placed a paw on the workbench as it lifted itself up on its two mechanical legs. It wobbled for only a moment before straightening completely.

"Hello, Mr. McClunkin. How are you today?"

The bear bowed deeply before straightening once again. "Hallo, Ms. Claudia. What can this fine bear do for you today?"

She smiled at her creation. For seven years she had worked at Industrial Toys. It had finally paid off. "Nothing for me, thanks. You are to be a Yule present for my brother Michael. Would you like that? I promise he will love you forever."

Claudia heard the bear's gears wind in excitement.

"First off, we're going to have to make you look like a proper present!" She ran into her mother's room and pilfered a length of green ribbon. She ran back to the automaton and quickly wrapped it around its shoulder and tied a largish bow. "Would you be so kind as to wait under the Yule tree until morning?"

"My pleasure, miss."

The bear hopped down off the workbench and scrambled out the door. She had no doubt it would find its way to the tree as she scrambled upstairs and into bed. She couldn't wait to see Michael's face in the morning.

Round Tom couldn't believe the streak of bad luck he'd been having. He had broken into four houses to steal Yule gifts, but not a one had anything worth taking. Obviously, he had picked the wrong part of London to begin his thieving career.

Getting laid off two weeks before Yule had been hard enough. Not that the lack of Yule presents bothered him, since he had none in the way of family. His worry was rent. His was due in two more days and unless he came up with it, he would find himself homeless and rupenceless on the streets. He really shouldn't have spent that week drinking heavily. He should have started thieving right away.

He decided to give it one more go. The house he spotted looked a *tad* more promising than the others. Unlike the Yule Father, he wouldn't be dropping down any flues. Round Tom was a locksmythe. He had been building locks for most of his adult life, and thus had gained the knowledge to open many, if not all, of them. It was this discovery that made him choose a career in thievery.

He slipped out his stolen toolkit and set to work on the meager lock separating him from his rightful due. In under ten seconds he had it unlocked and the door swung noiselessly open. Tip-toeing as quietly as a man of his girth could manage, he found the Yule tree in the family common room. He sighed in disgust. Less than a dozen shabbily wrapped gifts lay under the tin tree. *They couldn't even afford a real tree.*

He bent down and picked up the first gift, which rattled until something shattered. The rattles turned into the musical notes of broken glass *tinkling* inside the box. *Oops.*

He dropped it to the floor and picked up the second. Not taking any chances, he unwrapped it. A new cooking pot gleamed dully in the light of the fireplace. Round Tom rolled his eyes and hung it from the branches of the tree.

He fared little better with the rest of the gifts. Most seemed to be centered around a young boy. Tom grimaced. He had never gotten any presents as a child and he failed to see why this brat should be any better off.

He stomped on most of them, not caring if the family heard the destruction. They could be dealt with similarly. No one came down the stairs to see what the disturbance was. He knocked over the teddy bear and lifted his foot to deliver the crushing blow. The whiskey sodden synapses of Round Tom's brain fired off a message. *You can't stomp a stuffed animal.*

Tom smiled at his quick thinking. He set his foot down and picked the bear up. It was heavier than he expected, but incredibly soft. *Too, soft. Maybe a good singeing will roughen it up.*

He carried the bear over to the fireplace and tossed it into the fire. Or at least he tried to. The bear came to life mid-toss and grabbed Tom's wrist in its sharp little bear claws.

Blood spurted from the wound on his wrist. The bear let go and dropped to the floor as Tom grabbed the wound with his other hand to stem the flow of blood. Bear forgotten, he fell down on his large posterior and inspected the laceration.

It wasn't wide, but it was deep, almost bone deep. He needed a bandage.

A green ribbon, that would have done nicely, slipped over his head and pulled tight against his neck. He reached up with both hands, ignoring the pain in his wrist, and tried to slip his fingers under the green felt. He couldn't. He could feel the pressure growing and growing. He fully expected it to rip through his flesh at any moment, severing his head. Instead it loosened momentarily. Before he could rip it off, the bear spun around him, hanging on to the ribbon.

It deftly wound the fabric around his wrists, stopping the bleeding, but effectively tying his hands to his throat.

Helplessly, he stared at the bear.

"I am a present for Michael. I had to stop you from destroying me. You are a very bad man."

"I'm sorry," Round Tom sputtered, vowing silently to give up his life of crime.

"Since it is Yule, I accept your apology," the bear said and wandered off.

Round Tom breathed a heavy sigh of relief, trying to ignore the wetness in his trousers. With a heave, he pulled on his bonds, trying to free his hands so he could escape. No matter how hard he pulled on them, he had little luck extrapolating himself.

"Do you think you can untie me?" He called out to the bear, trying to see behind him. Surely the toy would let him go.

Sean Hayden

An odd crunching sound answered his question. It was followed by vast amounts of pain in his back and chest. He looked down at the red-hot fire poker sticking out of the front of his tweed jacket. A wet stain grew on his shirt as did the smell of smoke as the edges of the gaping hole still smoldered.

Limply, the bear pulled him over onto his side and stood in front of his face. "Your apology was accepted for the attempted thievery and destruction of the Yule gifts beneath the Withers' tree. However, I could not allow such a dangerous person around Michael. I must protect him with every weapon in my arsenal." The bear leaned over, only inches from Tom's face.

"I could have killed you with the poker. I intentionally missed your heart and heated it to cauterize the wounds. I'm afraid this is going to be a very painful lesson. Children must be protected at all costs. I do so hope we can be finished by morning. It is Yule, after all."

Round Tom felt the first incision of the bear's claws on the skin between his face and his hairline. He remained conscious as the bear slowly peeled back his scalp inch by inch.

By the time morning arrived, Tom realized the depth of his error.

I never really had a teddy bear growing up, I had a Mickey Mouse. I loved that damned stuffed mouse. Anyway, I write a lot of steampunk and horror. I thought it would be fun to combine the two for one of the shorts. Horrorpunk? Steamhorror? I don't know. All I know is I had fun writing this one and then hearing Jen say, "Ewww," when I was done.

~Sean

Jen Wylie

The Zombie Apocalypse

by

Jen Wylie

The Zombie Apocalypse
by Sara Johnson
April 22, 2023

For years, people made jokes about the Zombie Apocalypse. The internet was awash with funnies regarding what you should do and who to have by your side.

Zombie novels and movies gained in popularity, and not only in the horror genre. They entered young adult books and even romance. Where once people other than horror fanatics would shy away from anything zombie related, now the masses, even children, were inundated with knowledge and stories about them.

One would think when it actually came about people would have known what to do, at least the younger generations. Unfortunately the virus which created them spread at a rate which could not have been foreseen. Due to the type of medium by which it was transmitted, it was in fact, the young who succumbed first.

Few survived the Apocalypse. Fortunately the means by which the virus was first transmitted caused it to run its course more quickly. Many were infected in the first day and populations were totally decimated within the first week. Without brains to feed on, the zombies soon de-animated and became mere corpses.

Within a month the population of humans on Earth went from 7 billion to less than five hundred thousand. Those that survived, such as ourselves, lived in remote areas with no network technology. To this day communicative technology remains to be banned, due to the fear the Zombie Virus will reanimate.

Survivors continue to research, as safely as possible, how the virus spread so quickly. Records show devices themselves became infected and in turn spammed every device known to it. It was the first computer virus to not only infect computers, but also every other device connected by a communications network. What is not known is how the virus then transmitted to humans. Debate continues on whether it was created as such, the first virus meant to use technology as a host, or if this was the first case of techno-human mutation.

In either case, the Zombie Apocalypse was a sad time in human history. Particularly as the final thing many people saw was a link on their screen, "Want to see a Real Live Zombie?"

This flashy story was quite fun to write. Yes, I am making fun of how addicted we all are to our technological toys. Not that I can say much, I'm quite an addict myself. I'd write more here, but I have to check my various social media accounts.

~Jen

The Zombie Dialogues

by

Sean Hayden

"I can't believe you fucking shot me, you prick!"

"I hate to break it to you, Paul, but you're a zombie! Look at you, you sick son of a bitch. You're God damn rotting!"

Paul did indeed look down at the tattered remains of his red flannel shirt. Sure enough, where the buck shot had pierced his flesh, green blood oozed from the greyish skin covering his chest. "Ewww."

"You bet your ass, ewww. That's disgusting. Does it hurt?"

Paul looked up at his friend, Dennis, and thought about it for a moment or two. "No. Not at all. Weird. I guess I am a zombie. Funny though, I don't feel zombish."

Dennis cocked the shotgun, chambering another shell into the barrel. "You want to turn around and have me shoot you in the head, or do you want to see it coming?"

"What are you talking about, dickhead? I don't want you to shoot me at all."

"You're a zombie. You don't get a choice. You're not eating my brains, you sick fuck!"

Paul made a face at the thought of eating his best friend's brains. The thought turned his stomach more than a little. But then he thought about the size of the meal and raised his eyebrow. "If somebody tried to eat *your* brains, they'd surely starve to death, dumbass."

"Are you sure you're a zombie?" Dennis lowered the shotgun, but didn't close the distance between them.

"I think I am, now that you so rudely pointed it out, but I don't *feel* like a zombie. Does that make sense?"

"No."

"Okay. I'm rotting. I'm green. I just took a shotgun blast to the chest. These are all very zombie-like qualities. I'm sure if you were green, rotten, and full of holes, I'd be running around in circles screaming like a little bitch. My point is, I don't *feel* like a zombie. I can still talk. You ever heard a zombie talk?"

"No."

"Have you ever heard a zombie use logic to diagnose his illness?"

"No."

"Have you ever heard a zombie say anything?"

"Yes."

"What?"

"Brains!"

"That only happens in the movies, Dennis. Get real."

"No, then."

"See? I don't think I'm a zombie."

"What about *Serpent and the Rainbow?* He talked in that."

"Movie."

"Shit. I don't know. Maybe you aren't a zombie. What happened?"

"Was on my way home from Taco Bell and this dude jumped out and bit me. See?"

Dennis moved closer and looked at Paul's arm. A nasty, pus-filled bite mark decorated his friend's wrist. "Food poisoning?"

"Really? That's the best you can come up with?"

"It is Taco Bell. Who knows with refried beans?"

"Get serious."

"Rotting vampire?"

"I don't want your blood or your brains."

"Herpes?"

"Mutant herpes. Next?"

"Maybe your DNA kept you from going all zombie? Maybe you're a half zombie."

"Half zombie?"

"Yeah. Like a half vampire."

"You sure some zombie didn't already eat your brain?"

"I don't think so."

"I'm not so sure." Paul was done. He sat down on his friend's front porch and rubbed his face. Half of one cheek pulled away. "Shit."

"Want some glue?"

"No. Get me the stapler."

Twenty minutes later, they both sat on the porch swing. Paul's stapled cheek sagged a little lower than the other side. "Have you heard about anybody else getting bitten?"

"No. Nothing on the news either. I checked while I was getting the stapler."

"I'm thirsty."

"Beer?"

"Please."

"Be right back."

Paul waited for five minutes. Dennis never came back. He opened the front door and walked inside. Dennis' mother was hunched over her son and gnawing on his neck like a puppy with a bone. "Mrs. Johsnon?"

"Brains!"

"Son of a bitch. He was right." He walked over to his friend's mother and kicked her as hard as he could. Her head flew through the kitchen window. Her lifeless corpse fell on her son's unmoving chest. Paul pushed her away with his foot and leaned over his friend. He sat there unmoving until Dennis' flesh took on an unhealthy pallor and he started to stir.

"Brains?" Paul had meant it as a half joke, fearing he would have to kill his best friend just as he had killed his undead mother.

"Dude. You killed my mom."

"How do you feel?"

"I feel fine?"

"Dude, we're zombies!"
"No! We're un-zombies!"

I was stuck with what to write. Then I realized I wanted to have a little more fun...than usual with my writing. I took a couple of Beavis and Butthead retards, turned 'em into zombies, made them a little smarter than your average flesh eating ghoul, and *made a play on the title for The Vagina Monologues. I couldn't have asked for more. I really kind of like these characters and might continue their tale with The Zombie, Zombie Hunters... Then I'll let the reader's know what makes them special and not your ordinary run of the mill zombies. Give you something to look forward to if I continue on with the series.*

~Sean

Blue Moon

by

Jen Wylie

The witch bent over, picked up half of her face, and with a snarled curse stuck it back into place. Holding it there with one hand, she walked to the array of wicker cages at the side of the clearing. Words of power and magic flowed from her lips as she chose a small cage containing a chipmunk. With a bloody stomp and shouted word the magic settled about her, making her beautiful once more.

"Damned zombies," she muttered and then went back to work. The zombies she raised to attack a nearby village had been a great accomplishment. However they'd gotten a little out of control and one of the filthy beasts had bitten *her*. The outcome was more than a little unfortunate. She had a reputation to maintain after all.

The moon rose slowly. Despite her brief delay, she managed to have all of her preparations in order for the appointed time. Except for the broken cages and pile of dead animals off to one side, the clearing seemed serene and peaceful.

She settled herself down on the empty stone altar and closed her eyes. The power of the blue moon seeped down into her very bones. Wrapping the magic around herself, she pulled her soul free, leaving her body to stand before the matching altar next to hers.

It held the body of her identical twin sister. Pulling forth her magic, she activated a spell previously set in place. Power rumbled through the earth. Strange wisps of light formed between the altars. A moment later her sister's soul appeared.

Her sister frowned, looked around, and then up at the sky. "It's not time! What do you want, Emma?"

"Sorry to interrupt your vacation, Anna. I was worried about you. A Witch Storm blew through a few days ago and your spell might have become unstable."

"Oh." Her sister shrugged and smiled. "Easy enough."

Emma gestured to her body on the altar. "Does it seem alright?"

Anna barely glanced at it. Already murmured words filled the night air as powerful magic wrapped around Anna and the body. With a final shout she reached out and touched it, a snap of power zapping to her hand. Startled, she jerked back. "What?"

Emma smiled, holding firmly to the spell which kept her sister from seeing that the other altar contained her true body. "You'll be back at All Hallows then?"

Anna grimaced, looking around the clearing with sharp eyes once more before nodding. "The heat is nice, but some of the demons are tiresome."

"I'm sure they are."

"Shall I give Shaydren your regards?"

Emma growled as her sister smiled evilly and faded away. Back to Hell. Back into the arms of her demon lover. The demon who once belonged to Emma.

"Bitch," she muttered.

Inhaling a deep breath of cool air she forced herself back into a state of calm. One by one she set off the remainder of her spells. First, she bound herself to her sister's body. A body exactly like her own, but free of the zombie curse.

Slipping off the altar she stalked around the other, setting off the next spell. Thick bands of iron whipped out of the base of stone, snaking up and weaving a grate over the body. Another spell set it in place and made it stronger. No zombie or witch would escape it now. The next spell removed the soil under the altar. She smiled as it dropped into the hole, stepping forward to peer down.

"Good-bye, sister."

The last spell replaced the earth, effectively creating a lovely grave. When her sister returned she would find herself buried six feet under. Not that it would matter, since once she inhabited her body once more the stasis spell would end and the zombie curse would take over. Zombies didn't need to breathe.

Hopefully her sister appreciated all the effort she'd put in. Emma could only imagine how her sister would feel, the darkness, the pressure of the earth bearing down on her. The fear and horror when she realized she was a zombie. Maybe Emma would hear the screams as her sister was eaten alive by the curse. Slowly. She estimated it would be two to three months before the curse ate everything but the bones and then died. Her sister would get to go back to her lover in Hell again. Permanently.

She would be quite insane by then, too. "Will you still love her, my Shaydren?" Emma laughed. "I win."

I had the urge to write, I sooo wanted to write. A story for this anthology was on the top of my list but I was stumped. My brain was a frizzled mass of goo. I turned to facebook and asked for ideas–my only stipulation being they be paranormal and weird. What I got was zombies, a witch casting a spell on a cheating boyfriend, blue moon brings a wisp of strange light, and a twin haunted by another dead twin. Mashing those ideas all together, I came up with this story. I have to admit, it was super fun to do!

~Jen

Pumpkin Carver

by

Sean Hayden

I set down the poker without making a single puncture. I held the gutted gourd in my hands. I ripped off the folded paper taped to the front of it as my hand reached over to the kitchen table and grabbed the tiny little "saw" that came with the carving kit. You know the ones. Every September they find their way into every store across the country. The kits that turn un-artistic retards like me into pumpkin carving masters. I'd been using them for years. At first they delighted the neighbors and their kids with their intricacy. Now, everybody and their mother used them and the thrill was gone.

I sat alone, now that I was divorced and my kids were with their mother for Halloween. It was always much more fun doing this with them. They made me laugh and it was sort of a tradition with us. Traditions seemed to be the only thing we had left, anymore. Sure, they were different now, but clinging to that last bit of normalcy made things seem…well, more normal.

They were also my judges. I really did it for them. Every year I tried to outdo myself and make the coolest pumpkin ever. Now, they were trick or treating in a different neighborhood and carving pumpkins with their mother.

I plunged the saw into the orange flesh, intent on just carving out a simple face. Things didn't happen that way. I started thinking about everything that made Halloween special to me. The sights, the sounds, and the smells. Candy corn, autumn leaves, caramel. My hand flew steadily as I smiled and daydreamed of carnivals, vampires, Frankenstein, and witches.

At the end of my reverie, I finally looked. I couldn't identify any of the patterns I had wrought across the face of the pumpkin. What a waste. I had paid way too much for it at the church on the corner. What can I say, I'm still a sucker for Halloween. With a sigh, I went to set it on the counter to toss out later, but figured, "What the hell."

I carried it to the front porch and set it on the table by the door. Remembering the missing candle, I ran back into the kitchen and grabbed it from the bag the carving kit had journeyed home in. It was an orange pillar, probably too big for the job, but I was tired of replacing tea-light candles all night long. I walked back to the porch, stuck it in, reached into my pocket and grabbed my lighter to light it. I started humming the song from Phantom of the Opera (I have a Halloween snow globe that plays it) as I reached in and brought the pumpkin to life.

Without looking at it, I tossed the lid on and walked back into my lonely house.

It took twenty minutes for the first set of kids to ring my doorbell. Grabbing the bowl of candy, I twisted the knob and opened the front door.

A group of seven children stood transfixed by my haphazard creation. I gave them a strange look and coughed gently to herald my existence. As one, they turned and held out their bags. Each one of them was smiling.

"Trick or treat! That's an amazing pumpkin."

"Thanks," I said with little thought, kind of used to the compliments, even though they had faded over the years.

They turned back to the pumpkin before running down the lawn to the street. That piqued my curiosity. I reached inside and turned off the front porch light. Still holding the bowl of candy, I moved to stand in front of it.

My breath caught in the lump that formed in my throat. The bowl of candy fell from my hands and spilled against the fallen leaves that had gathered in front of my door. I had carved the tiniest lines in the flesh of the pumpkin. Without the wash of a glowing candle behind it, they meant nothing. A formless picture in ridged, lined flesh. With even the tiniest bit of illumination, they had flared to life painting a scene that thousands of words could never begin to describe.

I had painted art with a serrated blade.

A table, a father, two children, and a multitude of pumpkins. They were each jabbing their own pictures into the flesh. Carved out bits of pumpkin seemed to fly in every direction. If you stared long enough, the flickering of the flames almost brought animation to the tiny limbs and knives. On each tiny pumpkin face, past pumpkins of our endless tradition were spread out in a neat timeline. I recognized and remembered each one with a smile.

I stood there in the autumn night as tears fell silently down my cheeks. The breeze cooled them before they fell on my chest. With a silent thought I thanked the very holiday itself for all the memories that were so very precious to me.

I bent down and scooped the fallen candy into the empty bowl. I set it on the chair next to the table, went inside, and shut the door behind me.

Okay. This story is a little different for me. When I write, I never *have a plan. I rarely know what I'm going to do with a story or where it's going to end up. This one...yeah. It went in a completely different direction than I ever would have expected. My humor leaks into my writing. I can't help it. My* emotions *hardly ever do. Halloween has always been my favorite holiday, hands down. Even over Christmas. I love everything about it. I never delve into my personal life in my writing or in public. I'll be honest. Yes, I am going through a divorce right now. Yes, this is my first year without my kids. Yes, I see how I almost used this story as therapy. I'm sorry ~Insert blush here~, but to me it was too beautiful not to share. I don't know if you caught the other reference. The guy carving the pumpkin was me, sitting at the keyboard and telling the world how important his kids and all the things they used to do together are to him. This was just a tiny window into reality. Never let them see your weakness, but I'll be damned if by the time the main character shut the door, the tears on his cheeks matched the ones on mine.*

~Sean

Little Devil

by

Jen Wylie

As soon as Kevin got off the bus his mother knew she was in for a rough evening. From the living room window she watched him jump off the bus, not even taking the last step. He turned, gave someone the finger and then bolted toward the house, stepping in every puddle on the way.

Kevin was eight.

With a scowl she stomped to the door, ready to lecture him on the inappropriateness of such gestures. She just stepped into the foyer when he barreled by, almost knocking her over.

"Kevin!"

She turned to follow him and then stopped and let out a long irritated breath. Mud covered the floor, his shoes and jacket were tossed to the side, and his backpack upended, all of its contents strewn everywhere.

Yes, it was going to be a very long evening. Normally Kevin was a caring and sweet boy, but sometimes it seemed a little devil came home from school instead.

Kevin's mother tucked him into bed, early, and kissed his forehead. "Love you, sweetie. Tomorrow will be a better day. You just need some sleep."

With a huff he flipped over, putting his back to her. Mother was tough and hard to ruffle. She might frown and sigh a lot, but she never got really angry. When she threatened him, she actually did it too. He'd lost TV, video games, dessert, and been sent to bed early. It sucked.

The lights flipped off and his door closed. Kevin rolled over onto his back again and crossed his arms. This house was no fun at all.

Closing his eyes, he began to quietly chant.

When the strange words stopped, Kevin rested peacefully asleep. His body blurred and then a small, dark form rose up and swirled about until it stopped at the end of his bed and took shape once more.

"Maybe next time will be more fun, kiddo." With a smirk and a swish of his tail, the little devil dissolved into the darkness.

Little Devil

I'm the mother of two young boys. I think that is all the explanation I need on where this story idea came from. We all know our darlings are really always angels. Love you most, my babies.

~Jen

GTMV-219

by

Sean Hayden

I woke, and for the first time in my life I was thankful for that precious gift. One should never take waking up for granted. Normally, I stumbled around in a daze until about my fourth or fifth cup of coffee. This particular day, when my eyes snapped open, I sat up in bed and smiled. I never ever expected to live through the night.

Every test subject injected with GTMV-219 hadn't.

My father hadn't expected me to live, either. He had hoped...but I could see the fear in his eyes. Being your father's lab assistant had its advantages. It had some disadvantages, too, like accidentally taking a needle intended for a chimp.

"Dad?" I called his name softly, trying to wake him up gently. He sat in the chair next to my bed with a stethoscope still around his neck.

"James? You're ali–" At least he had the decency to look ashamed at his surprise.

"Yes. I'm alive. What happens next?"

I could see the wheels turning in his head. My father was one of the smartest people I had ever met or known. For him to not know an answer...it scared me more than a little. "Honestly, I don't know, son. The retro-virus in the serum was tailor designed for simian DNA. We share *many* genetic markers, but it's not an exact match. We'll have to watch you closely. Just be thankful you didn't end up like the others. Whatever happens, we'll fix it."

I nodded and swung my legs over the edge, letting my bare feet hit the cold linoleum of the lab room we had set up as a bedroom for the extraordinary long nights we sometimes pulled.

A horrible thought crossed my mind. In the six months I had been working with my dad, not once had I seen the results of any of the experiments. I helped with injections, care of the healthy animals, and some of the less classified paperwork. Once the chimps were injected, they were moved to another ward that I didn't have access to. I had asked to see the ward once and my father calmly shook his head and looked at me with sad eyes.

"Dad?"

"Yeah?"

"I want to know. What happened to the other test subjects? What does the virus do?" He started to shake his head again, and I slammed my hand down on the small end-table by the bed. "Damn it! This shit is in me now. I want to know!"

He let out a *very* resigned sigh. "Come on. I suppose it's pointless to keep it from you now."

He stood and waited for me to join him. As soon as I stood and stretched, he turned and exited the room. We made our way through the offices and labs I normally worked in until we stood before the sliding metal door at the end of the hall. Dad placed his hand on the reader and the door slid open with a quiet *whoosh.*

The smell of death nearly knocked me to my knees.

The hallway was black as night. Two swinging doors marked the end and eerie white lines shined through the miniscule space between the doors and beneath. I no longer had the urge to see inside.

"Come on, son."

I shook my head, but Dad grabbed my arm and gently pulled me along. I swear I could hear my feet screeching against the polished floor. "Maybe a quick debriefing of the results instead?"

He didn't utter a word and used one hand to push the doors open. Silence settled around us like a wet blanket as we walked into a morgue.

It looked like a zoo crime lab. Twenty ape corpses lined twenty metallic tables spaced evenly throughout the room. Some of the poor beasts were strapped to the tables, even in death. No two of them had died the same way. Some of them had died as their skin melted from their bodies, pooling on the tables around them. Some of them had jammed their own hands into their skull trying to end the pain. One had ripped its own limb off and still clutched it as it passed from this world.

I threw up on my father.

"What the hell, Dad? What were you trying to do?"

"Make the perfect man."

"Out of a monkey?"

"Chimp. They're more closely related to us."

"Why?"

"Because we're paid to."

My world came crashing down around me. I knew the chimps had died. As a student of science, I had come to accept that there would be losses for the betterment of mankind. It's one thing to accept those deaths and imagine them as a peaceful loss. To see the agonized looks and horrid deaths of the animals around me was something completely different.

"What if that had happened to me?"

"But it didn't. You survived."

"What if I turn into a fucking monkey?"

"It doesn't work like that. The retrovirus injection has but one purpose, to unlock the mutations already hidden within your cells. The virus itself, while intended for chimps, does not carry any simian DNA or anything like that. You're safe."

"Oh, goody," I managed to croak as I fell to my knees.

Suddenly I didn't feel so good.

I could feel my body heating up. I could hear my heart thudding in my chest more like a rabbit's heart than a humans. Cold sweat poured from every pore.

Fear seized me in its icy grip.

Surely if I were going to die, I would have done it last night. Maybe the chimp retrovirus just takes longer to work on humans?

I could hear my father calling my name, but it sounded hollow and almost echoed in my ears.

There wasn't any pain. I felt no desire to gouge out my eyes or rip myself limb from limb.

Then there was blackness.

"Is he alive?"

"The EEG shows minimal activity, his heart rate has settled around 220, but he is alive. I don't know how, but he survived."

I could hear my father's voice, clinical and detached. I had no idea who he was talking to though. I opened my mouth to speak and the shriek of some unknown animal erupted from my throat.

"He must be awake. Can he still understand us?"

"I doubt it. The boy has always been a disappointment. I'm surprised he understood me when he was human."

"That's cold, Charles. He is your son. When I said to proceed with human testing, I didn't mean on your family…"

"He was at hand, General. I made it look like an accident. He thought he did it to himself."

Any fear that had been left in my veins was replaced by hatred and anger. I tried to sit up, but I was strapped down like the other lab monkeys.

"He is impressive looking. Is that armor or skin?"

"It's chitin. When he collapsed, his skin turned almost translucent, and then darkened to black and hardened. Notice how the hinge of his jaw has extended to the facial armor? He is very impressive. Look at those canines. He could rip someone to shreds in moments. An army of these bullet-proof monsters would devastate any opposition."

"Can he fight though? We should test it against something. Maybe the one surviving chimp?"

"My pleasure, General. Amanda!" My father turned and looked for the other lab assistant. I had run into her occasionally. She had always been very distant, but nice.

"Yes, Dr. Blankenship?"

"Sedate him and put him in the hangar."

"Yes, Doctor."

I'd had enough. I pulled at my restraints. Nothing happened. I could feel them stretch minutely, but they wouldn't give. I tried pulling my arms up, but the hinged joints of my arms caught on the straps…

Inspiration struck. I pushed and pulled, pushed and pulled, dragging the rough edges of my hard exoskeleton over the straps of the gurney. I could *hear* them starting to fray.

"What's he doing?"

"Trying to escape. No worries, General. She'll be back with the sedative long before he escapes."

Overhead, a red light came to life, blinking in alarm. A claxon sounded as the doors of the lab closed and locked with a thunderous clang.

"Warning, the lab is in lockdown. All non-essential personnel are to vacate immediately," a computer generated voice sounded in the lab.

My father and the general hurriedly tried every exit from the cavernous lab to no avail.

The straps covering my chest snapped as my elbow finally sawed through.

The sedative never came.

This story was nothing but a mental exercise. When I write, I never plan on anything. I go into a story with a general, and I use the term loosely, idea and write around it. This time I sat down at the keyboard and let my fingers write the story. I had no idea where I was going with it, how it would turn out, or even who the bad guy would be. Hell, I didn't even know what it would be about. The plot unfolded as I typed and twisted and reshaped itself at least twenty times before it was through.

~Sean

Whisperings

by

Jen Wylie

They come in the night. These wild things. Whisperings in my mind.

They disturb my sleep, make me restless. I wish they would disappear. They don't. They have in fact, been growing stronger. I can't remember when they first started, little tendrils in my dreams. Several nights ago, maybe more. I can't think…I can't remember…

Tonight they are worse; growing bold, taunting me in the darkness. Restless, I toss and turn as if fevered. I'm not sick, I know I'm not. This isn't normal. They don't feel like dreams. If I open my eyes they're still there, dark shadows slowly invading my mind.

"Sleep," they whisper.

Always the whispers. I hate them. They tickle almost beyond my hearing. Nearly silent voices murmuring words in menacing tones. I find myself straining to listen, forcing myself to stop and then trying all over again. It is a vicious cycle I can't seem to stop. Perhaps that is their goal.

I'm so tired it hurts. I want to sleep so badly yet I find myself denying it to listen to the whispers. I need to sleep. I must force myself to ignore them. Though they whisper for me to do so, what they want is not the same. They aren't asking me to sleep like I so wish to. To fall into the deep slumber which leaves you healed and rested and ready to face a new day. The whispers are too wicked. Too laced with dark intent. The sleep they ask for is the eternal kind.

Somehow they read my thoughts, sending shivers of terror streaking down my spine.

"Sleeeep," the whisperings agree. "Just...let go."

I'm not ready for death. I'm too full of youth and life and want to live. I want to wake up. Or am I already awake?

Whisperings

The whisperings don't like such thoughts. Their mad mutterings increase, trying to drown out my treasonous thoughts. How many voices are there? I can't even count them they are so intertwined. They slip together and away, delving into my thoughts and seeking out every corner of my mind. There is no escaping them...no escape...

A whispered growl erupts through my mind.

I start awake so suddenly pain lances through my eyes. The sun has risen. As it breaks the horizon the whisperings fade, the dark tendrils recede. I don't even need to look at my clock. The memory that they do this every morning pushes through my weariness.

They are gone.

Or are they? Nestled under the blankets, my heart hammers against my ribs and my breath comes in shallow, frantic gasps. They can't be truly gone, because they keep coming back. Are they hiding? Sneaky little dark things masked deep in the corners of my mind? Or are they somewhere else close by? My gaze darts about the room, searching every shadow, every nook and cranny. There are too many shadows, too many places they could hide.

Frantically, I spring out of bed and start flipping on lights, running through the apartment turning every single one on. Will it help? I have no idea, but as I finally come to a stop in the small kitchen and flick the last switch the mind numbing fear recedes. My heart begins to slow. I can breathe again. Panic continues to tingle along my nerves. Sucking in a deep breath, I brush knotted hair from my face with shaking hands.

Coffee. That will help. Coffee makes everything better in the morning.

My little measuring spoon bangs around in the can as I jerk it from the cupboard. My hands are still shaking. I fumble with the stupid plastic lid. There isn't a lot left inside. I need to remember to put coffee on my grocery list. There's enough for a few more pots and that knowledge keeps me from panicking again.

Watching coffee brew is as bad as waiting for a pot of water to boil. It seems to take forever. I bite my nails and bounce in place impatiently. My thoughts are a scattered mess. Maybe there are time warps in kitchens. And waiting rooms. Time always seems to move slower there. The only thing I can concentrate on is getting some coffee into me. Finally there is enough for a cup and I steal it from the carafe. It will be strong, but I don't care. I'll add extra sugar.

Coffee is liquid life. Liquid calm. My hands finally stop shaking. My mind begins to settle. Taking fast, little sips, I burn my tongue and don't care.

The shrill ring of the phone startles me but I manage not to spill my coffee. I glance at the clock on the microwave and see I'm not yet late for work, but will be soon if I don't get my butt in gear. I grab the portable phone on my way out of the kitchen, wishing the intensifying headache behind my eyes would go the hell away.

"Hello?"

"Morning, sunshine!"

I bite my tongue on a sigh. "Hey, Mom." I speed walk back into the bedroom, eyeing up the shadows still present. They aren't moving, which is good. That I think they might, not so much. *Am I losing my mind?* I don't have time for irrational thoughts.

"Sweetie?"

"What?"

"I asked you how you're doing."

"Sorry, not awake yet." Setting the coffee cup on my dresser, I then quickly start to dig through the closet for clothes. "What's up?"

"Are you late?"

"Not yet. I'm getting dressed."

"Alright, sweetie. I just wanted to know if we're still on for tomorrow night?"

I pause in digging through my dresser for underwear. My memory clicks in. It's Tuesday. Wednesday is when my parents come over for dinner every week. "Yup. Any requests?"

The pause on the line makes my eyebrows go up while I wait. The correct and normal answer is no.

"Well," Mom finally answers. "Are you up for a few more guests?"

"Um, I guess?" I don't like where this is heading. I grab my coffee and take a frantic gulp.

I can almost hear Mom grinning. "Your Aunt Marsha and Uncle Ernie will be down. They'd love to see you–" My choking sounds make her stop. "You okay?"

Holding the phone to my chest, I cough some more and clear my airway. *Crap!* I can't stand my uncle. My aunt isn't much better. "Sorry, coffee went down the wrong way." My mind races, or tries to. It sputters, stalls and finally gives up. For the life of me I can't think of an excuse for them not to come.

The red lights of the digital clock by my bed catch my attention and I curse under my breath. "I gotta go. I'm going to be late."

"Wait!" Mom stops me before I hang up the phone. "Have you been sleeping okay?"

Her question catches me by surprise. My guard instantly goes up. Mom has a tendency to think anything wrong with me is caused by either the lack of a) proper diet and exercise, or b) a man.

"I'm fine."

She lets out a deep sigh. "Good, good. I just saw on the news last night–"

"I really need to go. I'll talk to you tomorrow, you can tell me then."

"Oh. Alright, sweetie. Have a good day! I love you!"

"Love you, too. Kisses." I make a few kissy sounds and hang up the phone.

My headache is now ten times worse. I squeeze my eyes closed and take slow breaths, wishing it would go away. Of course it doesn't. My eyeballs feel like they're on fire I'm so tired. *How am I going to make it through another day?* Yesterday had been bad enough. I'd wandered through the workday like a zombie.

Screw it. With a muttered curse I quickly dial the phone. "Hey, Brenda. Ya, I won't be in today. I think I've come down with something. Okay, yes. I'll let you know. Bye."

A deep breath shutters out of me. "That was painless." Now if only the pain in my head would go away. Work dealt with, I head for the bathroom for some headache meds.

The sight of myself in the mirror over the sink startles me so much I actually spill coffee. *Is that me? That can't be me.* Like an idiot I lean forward, peering into the bloodshot eyes of my image. Those eyes are sunken and ringed in black. My skin and lips are pale, almost waxy. My shoulder length, dark brown hair is a limp, tangled mess. I look half dead. I've never looked so horrible, not even back in my bar hopping days when I'd go many nights in a row with only a few hours of sleep.

"Jesus," I mutter. Leaning back I stare a moment more before grabbing the extra strength pills and popping two into my mouth, washing them down with my coffee. I hope they kick in soon. *Maybe I'm sick with something?* Other than being tired as hell and having a headache I don't feel like anything is wrong though.

Memories of the whispers come back. The darkness of them. The fear. My brows draw together and the face in the mirror grows even paler.

Are they nightmares? Did I just eat something bad? My reflection tells me no, they are something more. I haven't been sleeping…not at all.

I bite my lip. *For how long? How long has this been going on and I've not been remembering?* People can only go without sleep for so long. My exhausted brain tries to remember. I know going without sleep can cause hallucinations and paranoia. *Is that what's happening? Am I just imagining the whisperings?* But that doesn't explain *why* I'm not sleeping.

Wobbling a bit on my feet, I make my way to the kitchen and top up my coffee. My headache isn't going away. My eyes are still itchy and burning. I'm too exhausted to make my way back to the bedroom so I slowly make my way into the apartment's small living room and curl up on my favorite big chair.

Both hands around my coffee, I close my eyes and try to think. When was the last time I slept well? Not last night, or the night before. Not even over the weekend. My breath catches in my throat. I was tired most of last week as well. Have I been not sleeping at all this whole time? Or has it been a gradual thing? I don't know, and have no way of knowing.

"Shit."

I stare out the sliding glass doors that lead to a pitifully small balcony. In a daze, I sip my coffee until it's gone. Now I don't know what to do with myself. Glancing at the clock ticking away on the wall, I see almost an hour has passed. How did that happen?

Grimacing into my empty cup I struggle up out of the chair and shuffle into the kitchen. Once filled up again I decide to busy myself with dishes and cleaning. It's been a while since I'd scrubbed the counters, or the fridge. It's downright disgusting.

On my hands and knees I find cleaning the fridge comforting though. Maybe it's the bright light shining in my face. There are no deep, dark shadows inside. At the worst, just some bad cases of mold.

My muscles feel like jelly and I go through another cup of coffee by the time I finish. The microwave clock informs me I've spent most of the morning working away. Mission accomplished.

The exhausted feeling won't go away, but at least hasn't gotten worse. It worries me, I'd love to sleep, but my fear keeps getting in the way. "Shower time."

Pounding water makes me feel somewhat better. I crank it up as hot as I can stand it. I take my time. Once out and toweled off I moisturize and then use the towel to get as much water out of my hair as I can. I'm not a blow-drying girl. That just wrecks your hair something fierce.

The water relaxes and rejuvenates me. My mind is momentarily clear. I've been foolish. Sleep is what I need, I'm going to get some damn it!

Tossing on some sweat pants and a T-shirt I fall into bed and pull the covers up around me. I leave the lights on, which I normally would never do. I need dark, dark and quiet, to sleep. Usually.

Staring up at the ceiling, I just can't make myself close my eyes. I don't even want to blink. If I close them, will the whispers come? Even over the muted sounds of the city outside I can hear my heart pound faster and faster in my chest.

Tears pool and then slip down my cheeks. What the hell is wrong with me? I blink rapidly and brush the wetness away. *Think of something else. Think of something else. Don't think about the shadows.*

Shit.

Whisperings

With a not-so-muttered curse I toss sheets aside and scramble back out of bed. It's barely past noon. Standing so suddenly disorients me, my stomach flip-flops and the room spins. My eyes water and a headache starts to thump in my temples.

Maybe I should call and make an appointment with the doctor. I'd rather not, I can't afford it and they'd probably prescribe drugs out of my budget as well.

The reprieve the shower gave me was certainly short lived. I feel like crap again already. Wandering out of my room I stop in the kitchen to put on more coffee, then into the living room and plop into my comfy chair. I'll watch some mindless TV. Perhaps that will get my mind out of the darkness so I'll be able to sleep. Something needs to happen. I can't go on like this.

Cable quickly provides me with a bevy of shows each more stupid than the last. I'd forgotten how horrid the Networks' programming had become. People needed to be fired for airing this crap. Even so, it quickly takes my thoughts away. That is likely the intent, to make us all mind-numb zombies.

A flicker causes me to blink. I blink again and bolt upright. *Something is wrong...*

Everything flickers again. The TV makes a sharp pop sound and then fades black.

My increasing panic halts as a laugh skitters up my throat. *Just a power surge. The lights are still on. Everything's okay.*

A feeling of unease spreads through me. My lips tremble. I don't understand...

Suddenly nervous I glance to the patio doors. The blinds are shut. I stare at them uncomprehending. I never shut the blinds. I get up from the couch and freeze before I'm fully upright.

I hadn't been sitting on the couch...

Whirling around I look to my vacant comfy chair. A chill of fear courses over me, raising every hair on my body. Looking around I see only the lamp in the living room is on. All the other lights are off. Panic pushes me forward. Banging my shin on the coffee table doesn't slow me down. I run to the kitchen, flipping the lights on.

Disbelief holds me paralyzed. The coffee pot is empty. The carafe is washed and on the dry rack.

"Oh gods, no." Dashing to the cupboard I know what I'll find. The can is empty.

It hadn't been. "Oh no. No…no…"

My breath comes in panicked frantic gasps. I don't remember turning off the lights. I don't remember being in the kitchen. This is wrong, so very, very wrong.

Tears run down my cheeks as I grab my keys and purse from the counter and quickly unlock the door. Enough of this. I need to get out of here. I'll go see Mom and Dad, or my friend Jeannie or someone. Anyone.

Slamming the door closed behind me, I turn to lock it and then freeze. Slowly I look up and watch as each light down the long hallway goes out one after the other, dousing the hall in pitch black.

"You've got to be kidding me." Maybe I should still make a run for it.

In the darkness, something darker moves.

I'm back inside the apartment and locking the door behind me so quickly some of my hair gets caught in the door. I don't care. Once I'm safe, a savage pull frees me.

Tossing my things on the counter I run into the living room again and straight to the blinds. I fling them open… or try to. They don't want to move on their gliders.

Screeching in fear induced fury, I yank and pull until the whole contraption comes crashing to the floor in a jumbled mess. Chest heaving, I stare out at the darkening city.

"It can't be that late…" My head spins to the clock on the wall. Yes, yes it is that late. Very soon the sun will be setting.

Stepping over the mess of crumbled blinds I struggle with the sliding door until it finally whooshes open and I step out onto the small balcony. Crisp air envelopes me, drying the sweat of my fear and panic.

All around me lights are slowly coming on, more and more as the minutes pass. Calm begins to return. Cities are light. Light is safe.

I shift to be able to see past buildings to watch a little strip of yellow and pink sky slowly fade more and more as the sun goes down.

All around me the lights flicker again.

Gripping the railing like my life depended on it, my eyes search the streets and buildings, for what I don't really know.

Flicker.

The last of the light fades away. The sun has set.

Flicker.

For a moment, the city is completely silent.

Everything plunges into darkness.

My breath stops as my eyes fight to adjust. My heart feels like it's going to pound right out of my chest.

This was no little flicker. The lights don't come back. It's like I can feel everyone in the city, every single person, waiting…waiting.

Seconds tick by. They don't come back on.

In wild panic, I stumble back into my dark apartment as the screaming starts.

* * *

They love the dark, these things, these horrible whispers in my head. I know now I'm not alone, I've never been alone. I'm not the only one who has been subject to their maddening murmurs.

My body seems to go mad, banging around the room, knocking over furniture in its haste to…to what? I don't know. To escape the inevitable perhaps. My mind, my inner me…is quiet inside, watching. Not only watching, waiting. Not for the light like the rest of me, but for the whispers to make clear what it is they want.

They want me. They want me to sleep. What I don't know is why. What is their goal?

Their voices swirl around me, covering me in darkness from the inside out. They pull at my memories and innermost thoughts and feelings, pulling, tearing me apart bit by bit. Exhaustion has taken its toll on me. I'm too tired to fight. They know this. I think they may have even planned it.

"Yes, yes…" they agree.

I can feel what they say more than understand their muted, echoing words. Some people are stronger. Their minds more resilient. These people, these have known the whisperings for longer, these drew the whispering forth earlier than with the rest. The rest. *Everyone…*

"Everyone…each…and every…one…"

I come a bit more to my senses. Sprawled in my chair, I feel something warm on my face. Blood I think. Pain thrums like music throughout my body in tune to the melodious whispers. *What have I done to myself?* It's hard, so very hard, to think. Terrified and tortured screams echo into the room from outside. The whisperings grow more persistent in my mind.

"Sleep, sleep…let go…want…join us…feed us…sleep…weak…feed…sleep…let go…"

It's so hard to make sense of the words. They continue to tumble about, maddening in their existence and unclarity.

A whisper lashes out within me to be heard above all the rest. "Your time has come…"

Its tone is so deep, so inhumanly deep, my whole body vibrates.

"This day has been foretold…"

My heart shudders with each syllable as my back arches from the pain of the whisper.

"Humanity has had its time. It's chance…"

My hands clench and every muscle and tendon vibrates at a frequency too strong and deep to tolerate. A scream lodges in my throat, but it can't escape. I can't escape. I can't resist. I can't fight…

"It is time…to end."

The other whispers grow stronger, an insane and quiet babble overwhelming me.

Darkness overcomes me. Shadows swarm from everywhere, slipping dark and feathery over every part of me, filling me. I feel them under my skin, squirming in my eyes, pushing deep inside. They crawl down my throat, they steal my breath.

The deepest whisper speaks once more, and its words tear me apart, breaking me into dark little pieces.

"Sleep."

This story took the longest for me to write. It started as a nightmare I had during a very rough time in my life. I started writing it down to get it out of my head, and then it just got stalled when things got better for me. Eventually I did finish and I'm rather proud of my very first psychological horror. Though I will admit reading it again rather gives me the creeps.

~Jen

Bubba Fangs

by

Sean Hayden

It was a dark and stormy night. I looked up over the worn shelving. I had just put the last pair of size eleven work-boots we had in the stock room somewhat neatly on the top rack. Lightning raced across the sky like some sort of blue angled snake thing. I felt a shiver run down my back bone. I'd never been one for storms. Working the night shift at the SuperMart in the middle of one promised to make my work-day extra special.

I s'pose I should introduce myself. My name is Bubba, Bubba Hangs. I know what you're thinkin'. With a name like Bubba, I'm prolly one of them toothless SuperMart workers who don't know the difference between a shop-vac and a bag-less upright, but I do. My parents were firm believers in Missouri's education system. They made me stick with it. All the way through sixth grade!

I never did forgive them for that. Worst nine years of my life.

I'm not toothless either! I have all of 'em still. I brush them all the time. Most people say my smile is my best feature. I like to think my arms are. They're very big and I like to rub them with baby oil every day so they shiny. I even named 'em. Lefty and Righty. They do all sorts of cool stuff, like lifting…and breaking stuff. I'm pretty strong. My girlfriend says I smell that way, too. I don't get it. People actually smell strong?

The loud bang that usually accompanies the flashy stuff freaked me out a little. I couldn't take my eyes off the skylight in the ceiling. Whatever was going on outside wasn't good. I hoped we didn't get hit by a tornado. That would just suck. Well, maybe it would blow actually. Either way, I didn't like storms. When I was little, our house blew off its cinder blocks three times. Daddy had to call a crane truck to lift it back on. We were lucky. The other Winnebago's didn't fare so well. There's nothing like being asleep and getting thrown out of your bed in the middle of the night. People wondered why I hated storms so much. Well, duh.

"Excuse me, do you work here?"

The woman's voice behind me scared the living daylights out of me. I screamed like a little girl and Lefty and Righty went flying around on their own. I knocked more boxes of shoes than I could count onto the white linoleum floor. "Yes I do," I said and bent down to pick up the shoes.

"I'm sorry. I didn't mean to scare a big strong man like you."

"It's okay, ma'am. I don't particularly care for thunderstorms," I said and looked up.

I got past her black high-heeled shoes, up her calves, and to her knees before I took a big gulp of air. Most girls who came into the SuperMart didn't have legs like hers. They were silky and pretty. I forced my eyes to travel up farther and farther. She had on a skirt that looked like a belt. It barely covered what God had given her. Her blouse was completely see-through. Like those stockings you get in those funny plastic eggs on aisle six. Her hair was as black as night and her skin as white as a new six pack of underwear. She was beautiful.

"Where do you find the butcher section of this store?"

"It's in the back corner over there," I said, stood, and pointed, knocking another box of boots on the floor. I left it there with the others. "Would you like me to show you?"

She seemed to think about it for a moment. She looked like she was going to say no, but she smiled and nodded. "That would be delightful."

I grinned. "Follow me, ma'am."

I took her down the rest of the shoe aisle, and cut across home-furnishings. We emerged in the frozen foods section. I turned to wait, but she stood less than a foot behind me. "The butcher block is right over there," I stuttered and pointed.

"Is there a restroom around?"

"Over by sporting goods."

"Could you show me where that is instead?"

"I have to go pick up those–"

I stopped midsentence. The words just died in my mouth.

"Could you show me where that is instead?"

"Sure, follow me…" I turned and headed toward the land of firearms and hockey sticks. I knew I had to go clean up all the work-boots I had dumped, but suddenly I didn't care. All I cared about was helping my new friend.

It took us only a few minutes to navigate the store. We slipped into the hallway with the huge *Layaway* sign over it and again I pointed, this time at the ladies restroom.

"Would you give me a hand? I don't like touching public restrooms."

"Sure thing, miss." I pushed open the door and held it open for her. She stepped inside and looked at me over her shoulder.

"Any one of the stalls will do. Open the door for me."

"Chu got it, ma'am." I chose the one farthest from the entrance. Most people didn't like to walk that far, so I figgered it would be the cleanest.

She slid inside. I gave her a big grin. Being raised by my Mama taught me some manners. I made to pull the door shut behind her…give her a little private time. She spun around and her hand moved so fast I didn't even see it! Her fist wrapped around the buttons of my polo shirt and she yanked me inside that stall faster than you could say, "Red-light special."

I gulped as she wrapped herself around me. I shore never had a girl take such an interest in me quite that fast before. I brought Betty, my current girlfriend, flowers every night she worked at the bowling alley for six weeks before she even let me take her to the movies!

My new friend slid her knee up the outside of my leg as she pulled me down to kiss her. I closed my eyes and stuck out my lips and waited…

Her laughter broke my concentration. I opened my eyes to see what she was laughing at when I felt a *really* bad pain in my neck and a loud, wet crunching sound. I opened my mouth to holler when the funniest thing happened. The pain turned into…um…let's just say it gave me a funny feeling in my…um…tummy. I think I dropped to my knees. I can't really remember that part. The only thing I *do* remember is lying down on my back, the purdy little lady sitting on my chest, and shuddering like one of those funny flashlights (at least that's what Mama used to call it) Mama used to keep in her drawer. Then…nothing. I must have blacked out

It was a dark and stormy night. To top it all off, I woke up on the floor in the shitter of Supermart. Some nights I really hated my job. I said, "Ewww," as I touched the floor while I lifted myself up.

There was no sign of the woman who had kissed me into a nap. I wasn't surprised. I prolly dreamed the whole thing. Girls like that couldn't be real. Not at Supermart. Girls like that hung out at the mall. I stepped out into the empty (Thank Baby Jesus) restroom and quickly washed my hands before hightailing it back to shoes and men's wear.

"Bubba! Where have you been?"

My shoes screeched against the grey linoleum as I skidded to a stop. My boss, Violet, didn't like me very much. I had no idea why. I'd never done anything to her. Well, I did throw up on her shoes one time, but that was when I first started. I'm pretty sure she should have been over it by now. "I'm sorry, Violet. I did a restroom check, slipped, and banged my head. I must have knocked myself out."

She looked at me all skeptical like. She raised one of her violet (she died them to match her hair and her name) eyebrows. I don't think she bought it. "Somebody made a mess in the work boots. Go clean it up," she said and held her hand up to me as she walked away, probably to go torment the girls on the registers.

I shook my head and went to do as I was told. I made it to the pile of boots and boxes and bent over to pick them up. Bending over wasn't such a good idea! My stomach felt like I ate a week old 7-11 burrito stuffed with Poprocks (yes, I am speaking from experience).

I stood as quickly as I could, hoping I just pinched something, but it only got worse. I lifted up my hands and grabbed the shelf in front of me to ride out the gut bomb. My stomach sounded like blue whales singing karaoke while being auto-tuned. It wasn't pretty or harmonious.

Then came the rumble…

I knew I had only moments before my cheeks (the southerly ones) unleashed a torrent of holy hell the likes of which this planet had never seen.

That's when things got a little…weird.

I took off a runnin'. I've never been a fast runner, but holding my butt cheeks I took off like a cheetah with a bottle rocket stuck in its tailpipe (if you know what I mean). Lightning flashed and it seemed to stop. It illuminated the motionless people as I made my mad dash to the indoor outhouse. I moved so fast time stopped tickin'.

I kicked open the door, dropped my britches, and twisted in the air as I jumped through the nearest stall. My ass discharged just as I made contact with the cold plastic of the turlet. I'd never said, "Thank you, Jesus," so many times since the first time I got lucky with Loucinda Lou (don't judge me, she's my *third* cousin).

The gut bomb turned into full blown intestinal thermonuclear warfare. There were no survivors. The bathroom would have to be sealed off for ninety years until the fallout dropped to habitable levels. They would have to issue radiation suits to the janitors.

Waves of searing pain hit me everywhere else. My skin felt like it was on fire. I could hear my heartbeat in my ears. I didn't *really* start to panic until I noticed it was slowing down after each beat. As breathing became difficult, my heartbeat stopped altogether.

My very last thought was, "Workman's comp."

The last thing I ever expected was to wake up. Of course it had to be in the Supermart shitter again. Why couldn't I wake up in my bed like normal people?

My pants were still around my ankles and I was leaning against the silver metal pipe with the flushy handle. It wasn't the most comfortable of positions. I sat up and saw my skin.

Mama had a bit of Cherokee in her veins from way back. We didn't look like Native folk, but it did add a bit of color to our skin and made tanning unnecessary. It was gone. All gone. I looked so white I was almost blue. I could see every vein beneath my skin like a tiny blue river. I shrugged and then I remembered. I had died. No wonder I was blue.

I wiped my posterior and pulled up my Levi's. Without looking, I reached back with my foot and kicked the handle on the toilet. Whatever my body had gotten rid of was now gone forever. I stepped out of the stall and stood in front of the sink to wash my hands. The normally cold water felt pretty warm against my skin. I shrugged and reached for the soap dispenser. Normally you have to push pretty hard to get it to squirt some foam. One push and the thing exploded against the beige tile.

I was covered in soap and plastic. But that was the least of my problems. I caught my reflection in the mirror. I looked twenty pounds lighter (not surprising, I prolly crapped that much). My face was thinner and more angular. My eyes used to be blue. They looked like someone had bleached them and then put glow-in-the-dark contact lenses in them. I opened my mouth to say, "WTF," but as soon as I saw my teeth, I knew exactly what had happened. I'd seen enough horror movies. That lady wasn't a lady at all. She was a vampire. A bloodsucker. And now I was too.

The door to the restroom kicked open.

"Bubba...you had better not be hidin–there's your dumb ass. Listen to me..."

Violet had barged into the men's room like she owned the place. I saw her in the mirror as she saw me standing there. A hunger started in my stomach and I could feel the saliva gathering in my mouth like someone had dropped a T-bone right in front of me. It wasn't steak I wanted. I wanted something a little more purple...Violet even (see what I did there?).

"Hello, Violet."

"Bubba...f-f-fangs," she said in a whisper.

"Bubba Fangs. I like that," I said as I tore her throat out with my new teeth.

I sat down to write a story. Now before that ever *happens, the author's first rule of thumb is...check facebook. Well, lo and behold, one of my favorite topics graced my timeline! Yep, you guessed it...The People of Walmart! Walmartians are always good fodder for stories. Then I thought, what if one of them became a vampire! Yes! Winner winner chicken dinner!*

~Sean

Duck Hunting

by

Jen Wylie

Marlene started awake at the sudden sound of gunfire. Pops and bangs echoed repeatedly, jarring her teeth and starting an immediate headache. Cracking open an eye, she glanced at the clock. It wasn't even six yet.

"Oh, seriously guys."

Another wild round went off.

"What the hell!"

Marlene rolled over in bed to look at her best friend who'd stayed the night for a sleepover. Candy's curly hair was a wild mess around her wide-eyed face. She looked like she'd been electrocuted in the night.

"Go back to sleep," Marlene muttered, hiding a small smile.

"What's going on?" The gunfire was still going strong.

"Either the zombie apocalypse has started…or duck hunting season just opened."

Candy groaned and fell back, pulling her pillow over her head. "Why do they have to start so damn early?"

The shots stopped and they both breathed a loud sigh of relief and then laughed. When the shots started in a frenzy again they groaned in unison.

Candy threw her pillow at the window. "Damn it! How many ducks are there? Don't they have limits or something?"

"I'm thinking it's more likely they're just crappy shots." Marlene stretched and then left the warm safety of the blankets.

"What are you doing?"

"Closing the damn window," she said as she made her way across the cluttered floor of her bedroom. "Hopefully that will help."

Her window was wide open and she paused when she reached it as the shots once again stopped. Dad had already taken the screens out for the winter on the weekend. They'd had a nice cold spell that thankfully cleared out the last of the mosquitoes. The sun had barely risen. Outside it seemed only the sky was lit with gold and pink and rest remained in darkness.

The shots started again, though fewer and more sporadic this time. Someone hollered in the distance. Maybe they'd finally gotten one and would stop now. She doubted she'd be so lucky. Cursing under her breath she reached up to the pull the window down.

Rotting arms shot through the window, grabbing her arms and yanking her out with supernatural force. She barely got a scream in before the zombie ripped her face off.

Duck hunting season didn't start for another week.

Duck Hunting

Whatever could have sparked this story you ask? Well, actually it was 7am when the stupid hunters started. I hope they didn't get anything. My sleep is precious to me. I guess I'm going to have to start sleeping with my window closed again...

~Jen

In Hell

by

Sean Hayden

I remember the slurping noise as the son-of-a-bitch pulled the knife from my chest. I looked down and felt the blood soaking into my clean white shirt before I saw it. The stain spread as I fell backward striking the cold damp pavement beneath me. My head made a sickening sound as it struck last.

I felt the thief digging through my pockets as I took my last few breaths. His blade must have nicked my heart instead of piercing it, otherwise I probably would have remembered nothing.

I looked up at the streetlamp overhead. Its glow seemed to spread as a tunnel opened up in the sky above me. I pulled myself up out of my body and looked down upon my physical form, one last time. Memories of a wonderful and bittersweet life flashed through my head as every emotion I had ever felt washed through my soul. I cried and laughed, sobbed and smiled as I turned to let the light take me away.

I traveled for only a few moments before the tunnel split. One branch pointed straight up and was lit with a brilliant blue light. The other pointed straight down and was awash in a flickering orange. It was a no-brainer.

As soon as I hit the fork, I willed myself to go up. It worked for a few moments, but then spiritual gravity took over as I plummeted downward. I guess I shouldn't have been surprised. I always knew I'd end up in hell. I just hoped they had a smoking section.

It's not that I was evil or a bad person either. I knew the world had to have been created by a god. I knew it in my heart. Nothing that perfect could be accidental. My problem is that I never made a choice. Religion scared me more than the thought of hell. There was no happy medium with any of them, except maybe Buddhism and Wicca.

They did appeal to me, but my problem was me telling people I was a Buddhist or witch. *Hmmmm. Long haired white guy. Sure you are.*

So, instead of focusing on a religion, I focused on logic and just being nice when I could. I hoped if there were a heaven or a hell it would be enough to buy me a ticket into the good spot. I guess I was wrong.

The journey down didn't take too long. I landed face first in a field of burning grass. It didn't hurt like you would expect a mile long fall would. I just stood up and dusted myself off and put out the flames that had ignited on my shirt and jeans. People were landing all around me and doing the same. The look of utter fear and surprise on their faces kind of made me giggle. *Dumbasses.*

Something pulled me forward. I figured I might as well get this over with. If I was going to burn for all eternity, might as well get on with it.

We all walked for miles and ended at a gate of bone. It was creepy, I'll admit, but in a Halloweenish kind of way. I liked it. A few cobwebs and the place would be quite festive.

"Mr. Hayden."

I looked up and saw a figure dressed in a black, hooded cloak. *Shocker.* "Yes. That's me."

"I know. It wasn't a question."

"Oh, sorry."

"I know that, too."

I couldn't help it. I laughed. He didn't seem surprised by that, either. I guess it would be hard for a skeleton to look surprised. I knew I was standing before the Grim Reaper himself. I felt almost honored. I wondered, briefly, if he would be offended if I asked him for his autograph.

"Offended, no. Amused, no. Come on, you have a busy day ahead of you."

To my surprise, he left his podium of bone. He held out a skeletal hand to me and I shrugged as I reached out and took it. I'm sure by the end of eternity I would be touching many more things that would be classified as "ickier than a skeleton hand".

"You'd be surprised," he said.

Can he read everybody's thoughts?

"Yes."

I decided not to think. It had always worked well for me in the past.

He led me through hell. Just like in the stories, there were different hells for different sins. Gluttons were chained before magnificent feasts as hunger clawed their bellies like angry demons. Wanton men and women engaged in a frenzy of sexual acts with no hope of release. Angry people shouted with no voice, people were forced into manual labor, once beautiful people were horribly scarred, and the once wealthy were stripped of all their possessions.

Everybody had their own personal hell.

I briefly wondered what mine would be.

For once, Death didn't enlighten me. The suspense was killing me.

He opened a giant set of double doors festooned with writhing corpses held in place with thick wooden stakes. "They thought it would be fun to keep people locked away. Ironic isn't it."

I nodded.

"That's all hell is really. The final irony. You spend eternity living out the antithesis of your existence."

"Do a lot of people go to hell?" I couldn't help but ask.

"Very rarely does a soul make it to heaven anymore."

"But why?"

"Every religion has basic tenets. Have you ever noticed a similarity between them all?"

"Thou shalt not?"

"Pretty much," Death responded.

"So all those silly rules about gay people and tattoos were real?"

For the first time, I heard Death laugh, before answering, "Yes."

"So God really hates gay people?"

"Of course not!" He slapped me in the back of the head for good measure.

"Then why?"

"Because they believed. They believed that being gay was a sin. That was in their book of rules. Thou shalt not commit adultery...thou shalt not covet thy neighbor's wife...thou shall not...not...not. The list is quite extensive. They focused on the ones they would never break and totally disregarded the rest."

I understood exactly what he was saying. It was your own beliefs that set the parameters of your sins. *But what about me?*

"Your lack of beliefs kept you from heaven. But your lack of beliefs also keep you from being punished. Congratulations. You're hired."

Can I be frank? No? Okay then, I'll just be Sean. I'm warning you though, you shoulda let me be frank. Things are much less crazy around here when I get to be frank. Want to know the inspiration to this story? Facebook. Again. I got into a huge argument with a childhood friend who also happens to be a conservative Christian. I have a lot of friends who are gay. I firmly *believe with all my heart and soul that if two people are in love, they should have the* exact *same rights as any other two people who are in love. I don't care what combination of penises or vaginas they have. People are people regardless of gender. When people quote the bible to me how homosexuality is a sin, I usually point out to them that the bible says tattoos are a sin, as well as cheating on your spouse, coveting thy neighbor's wife or possessions, taking God's name in vain, and that it's okay to kill a woman on her wedding night if she's not a virgin. That usually shut's the smart ones up. The dumb ones keep going...*

~Sean

Shadow of Innocence

by

Jen Wylie

She stands in the center of the vale. Her long, dark hair flows unbound behind her, dancing in the faint breeze. Her simple homespun dress covers a figure fully curved, yet slim with youth and health. Innocence radiates from her, pulling, tugging us ever closer.

We can't resist. It is against our nature to do so.

Because of this so many of the herd has fallen. The innocence of her youth and virginity still outweighs the many deaths she has caused.

Watching from the cover of the woods surrounding the vale, more and more of my herd arrive. Each one struggles to resist. So far, none have broken from the shadows of the trees and gone to her.

Yet.

One will, eventually. They will lose the battle against their nature. We are kind, loving creatures. Purity is part of our nature. Innocence is impossible to resist, pulling us like a moth to a flame. In this case, the result is the same. Our numbers have dwindled considerably because of her over the past year. Gone were the times when maidens would lull us into their laps and bind us with silken bridles to capture us. Then, they would lead us to their villages to cleanse poisoned wells and heal the sick before releasing us back into the wilds. Not so anymore. The humans have grown greedy.

For the first time, I understand the feeling of hate. The love for my herd rises above the desire to bask in her innocence.

Next to me, Meren steps forward. I shoulder her aside with an angry snort. She is young and would certainly not be able to escape.

I will go.

The herds' dismay and fear echoes through my mind. It strengthens me as I step forward into the midday sunshine flooding the vale. The breeze ruffles my mane and the makes the bright flowers and grasses dance around my golden hooves.

A smile spreads across the girl's face as she sees me. Her arms spread wide, beckoning me closer.

It is a shock to so suddenly find myself only a few feet away. Stopping physically pains me. The need to kneel before her, to rest my head in her lap, is overwhelming. Despite knowing my death awaits me if I fail to resist her, my resolve waivers. I cannot do this. I cannot fight her.

Closing my eyes, my head lowers.

This close, her innocence is not quite so overwhelming. It takes me a moment to recognize the other feelings emanating from her. Greed. Anger. Hate.

My ears swivel. I hear the men hiding in the woods behind her readying themselves to kill.

She is not as innocent as she should be.

For the love of my herd, neither am I.

My muscles tense a moment before I lunge forward. The humans do not expect it. Head still bowed, my golden horn pierces her chest. A startled gasp is the only sound she makes before she dies. My head bows further; in remorse, in anger, in despair. Her body slips from my horn to land in a heap on the flowered ground.

Men burst from the woods, swords drawn, screaming in anger. *Are they angry over her death or that she failed to lull me and take my life*? I do not know. Humans are curious creatures I've never fully understood. Anger overwhelms my curiosity.

They have stolen so much that is pure and good in the world by taking our lives. They have desiccated our bodies, cutting us into bits, selling our horns and hide, bones and blood. And to what end? What foul magics have been cast? It is no wonder the world is falling into darkness.

Despite the girl's death, they are not prepared for me to fight. With horn and hoof I bear down on them in a fury. These humans have been destroying my herd. My family.

They have never seen the fury of a unicorn. To them it is an impossibility. It seems only moments pass before all have fallen. Dark human blood runs down my horn, is spattered across my body and up my legs.

In the sudden quiet the herd moves slowly into the vale to surround me.

I am uncertain how they will respond to such violence. Raising my head proudly, I stand firm in the knowledge that today I protected them.

One by one, they lower their horns to the ground.

Raising my head higher, I rear up. My actions have not been questioned. The violence and blood may disagree with them, but they understand.

Turning, I catch sight of something that causes me to stop in my tracks.

No longer is my hide the purest white.

Darkness fills my vision. My coat is now pitch black. As are my once golden hooves and horn. My fury and violence has changed me into something else. A black unicorn. One who will fight. One who will kill.

Perhaps there is hope for us after all.

What now?

I have sacrificed my purity for my herd. I am no longer fit to lead them.

Sallian steps forward, regarding me warily. Raising my head, for a moment I stare him down. With a snort I finally look away. For centuries I have led the herd. I know it is not something I can do now. Sallian is strong and intelligent and has tested me well in the past. He will lead them well.

He turns his head to regard the carnage in the valley. *We will need to move, Eirinar. There will be repercussions because of this.*

Looking back at him, I nod. I do not lower my head in shame or regret my rash actions. I did what needed to be done. Thankfully I feel the herd has no anger or hate for what I have done. There is only sadness and remorse.

I sense Sallian's hesitation. *You will be welcome among us.*

His words surprise me. I cannot accept. Not now. Perhaps not ever. I feel…I do not wish to taint the herd with violence and fury. With death. Even so, I bow my head slightly to acknowledge the offer. *I will guard your departure. When you need me, I will be there.*

Sallian nods once his understanding and then lowers his horn to the ground. The rest of the herd gathers around me and does the same. One last homage to their old leader. My heart pounds within my chest as pride fills me. While I led them, I did well. In the end…I gave them everything.

They rise as one. Sallian turns swiftly, leading them into the woods and north to safety.

I stand alone in a vale of blood and death. Already the buzz of flies tickles my ears and the shadows of circling carrion birds dance across the ground.

Closing my eyes, I try to settle my thoughts and heart. I did what needed to be done. The herd is safe and will remain so as long as I live. I will follow them and protect them as I didn't do before. As I couldn't do. Quite likely I will not survive long. Yet perhaps I will. Time is on my side. I will learn quickly to survive, to hunt, to kill. To be the hunter instead of the prey.

I have changed so much already. Never before would I, would any of my kind, have had such thoughts. My heart lifts. It is better this way. Now, I am more than I ever could have been. I will be a shadow to their light, always there to guard and protect their innocence. I will keep them safe. No longer will humans hunt us or have maidens lure us to our deaths. I will be a shadow in the woods hunting *them*.

Perhaps one day they will learn to respect us once more. Maybe, they will even learn all they ever needed to do was *ask*.

This story just popped into my head one day. I've always loved unicorns. When I was little I had stuffed ones, unicorn bed sheets and a collection of figurines. I've read a number of stories about unicorns over the years, and it always bugged me how maidens had such control over them. A number of stories not even unicorn related speak of unicorn horns (as ingredients, items of power etc). Horns no longer attached. So here is a story where these magnificent creatures stand up for themselves!

~Jen

Other Works by Jen Wylie

Flashy Fiction and Other Insane Tales (Anthology)

The Broken Ones
    -Broken Aro (novel)
    -Broken Prince (Coming Soon)

Sweet Light (novel)

Ring Around the Rosie (short story)

Jump (short story)

Immortal Echoes
    -The Forgotten Echo (novella)
    -The Untouchable Echo (short story)

Tales of Ever (YA novella series)
    -Banished
    -Fire Girl
    -Shadow Boy
    -The Lost Tree
    -Dragon Rising
    -Sanctuary

Jen Wylie's Biography

Jen Wylie resides in rural Ontario, Canada with her two boys, Australian shepherd, and a disagreeable amount of wildlife. In a cosmic twist of fate she dislikes the snow and cold.

Before settling down to raise a family, she attained a BA from Queens University and worked in retail and sales.

Thanks to her mother she acquired a love of books at an early age and began writing in public school. She constantly has stories floating around in her head, and finds it amazing most people don't. Jennifer writes various forms of fantasy, both novels and short stories.

Find out more about Jen at www.jenwylie.com and follow her on twitter @jen_wylie

Other Works by Sean Hayden

The Demonkin Series:
- -Origins
- -Deceptions

Rise of the Fallen:
- -My Soul to Keep

The Magnificent Steam Carnival of Professor Pelusian Minus Series: (Co-authored with Connor Hayden)
- -First Flight
- -Second Chance
- -Third Time
- -Fourth Stand

Lady Dorn

The Games We Play

Her Majesty's Mysterious Conveyance (Anthology)
- -Queen of the Travelers

The Ghost of Christmas Last

Flashy Fiction and Other Insane Tales (Anthology)

Sean Hayden's Biography

Born the son of a fire chief, Sean naturally developed a love of playing with fire. His family and friends quickly found other outlets for his destructive creativity. Writing is his latest endeavor.

Always a fan of the macabre, mythical, and magical, Sean found a love of urban fantasy and horror. After writing several novels in this genre, he found, fell in love with, and immersed himself in steampunk. He has always wanted to rewrite history and steampunk gave him that opportunity.

Sean currently lives in Florida as a fiber-optic engineer as well as an author. He was blessed with the two most amazing children he could ever hope for, has met the absolute love of his life, who coincidentally is his partner in everything. His hobbies include grand designs on world domination as well as a starring role in his own television sitcom.

www.seanhayden.org